THE BEGUM'S FORTUNE

JULES VERNE

WILDSIDE PRESS: MMIII

A STRUGGLE FOR LIFE. [*Page* 140.

CONTENTS.

LIST OF ILLUSTRATIONS.

Published by
Wildside Press
P.O. Box 301
Holicong, PA 18928-0301 U.S.A.
www.wildsidepress.com

THE BEGUM'S FORTUNE.

CHAPTER I.

ENTER MR. SHARP.

" REALLY these English newspapers are very well written,"
said the worthy doctor to himself, as he leant back in a
great leathern easy-chair.

Dr. Sarrasin had all his life been given to soliloquising,
one of the many results of absence of mind.

He was a man of fifty, or thereabouts ; his features were
refined ; clear lively eyes shone through his steel spectacles,
and the expression of his countenance, although grave, was
genial.   He was one of those people, looking at whom one
says at the first glance, " There is an honest man ! "

Notwithstanding the early hour, and the easy style of
his dress, the doctor had already shaved and put on a
white cravat.

Scattered near him on the carpet and on sundry chairs,
in the sitting-room of his hotel at Brighton, lay copies of
the *Times*, the *Daily Telegraph*, and the *Daily News*.   It

B

was not much more than ten o'clock, yet the doctor had
been out walking in the town, had visited an hospital,
returned to his hotel, and read in the principal London
journals the full report of a paper communicated by him
two evenings previously at a meeting of the great Inter-
national Hygienic Conference on the " Compte globules du
sang," or " blood-corpuscle computator," an instrument he
had invented, and which even in England keeps its French
name.   Before him stood a breakfast-tray covered with a
snowy napkin, on which were placed a well dressed cutlet,
a cup of hot and fragrant tea, and a plate of that buttered
toast which English cooks, thanks to English bakers, can
make to perfection.

" Yes," he repeated, " these journals are really admirably
well written, there is no denying the fact.   Here is the
speech of the president, the reply by Doctor Cicogna of
Naples, my own paper in full, all as it were caught in the
air, seized and photographed at once !

" Dr. Sarrasin of Douai rose and addressed the meeting.
The honourable member spoke in French, and said, ' My
auditors will permit me to express myself in my own
language, which I am sure they understand far better than
I can speak theirs.'

" Five columns in small print !

" I cannot decide which reports it best, the *Times* or the
Telegraph, each seems so exact and so precise."

Dr. Sarrasin had reached this point in his meditations, when one of the waiters of the establishment, a gentleman most correctly dressed in black, entered, and presenting a card, inquired whether "Monsiou" was "at home" to a visitor.

This appellation of "Monsiou" the English consider it necessary to bestow indiscriminately on every Frenchman —in the same way they would think it a breach of all the rules of civility did they fail to address an Italian as "Signor," and a German as "Herr." Perhaps on the whole the custom is a good one—it certainly has the advantage of at once indicating nationalities.

Considerably surprised to hear of a visitor in a country where he was acquainted with no one, the doctor took the card, and read with increased perplexity the following address :

> *Mr. Sharp,*
> *Solicitor,*
> 93, *Southampton Row, London.*

He knew that a "solicitor" meant what he should call an "avoué," and signified a lawyer of the compound nature of attorney, procurator, and notary.

"What possible business can Mr. Sharp have with me ?" thought the doctor. "Can I have got into some scrape or other without knowing it ? Are you sure this card is intended for me ?" he asked.

" Oh yes, Monsiou."

" Well, let the gentleman come in."

A youngish man entered the room, whom the doctor at once classed in the great family of " death's heads." Thin dry lips, drawn back from long white teeth, hollow temple-bones, displayed beneath skin like parchment, the complexion of a mummy, and small grey eyes as sharp as needles, quite justified the title. The rest of the skeleton, from the heels to the occiput, was hidden from view beneath an ulster, of a large chequer pattern ; his hand grasped a patent-leather bag.

This personage entered, bowing in a hasty manner, placed bag and hat on the ground, took a chair without waiting to have one offered, and opened his business by saying—

"William Henry Sharp, Junior, of the firm of Billows, Green, Sharp and Co. Have I the honour of speaking to Doctor Sarrasin ?"

" Yes, sir."

" François Sarrasin ?"

"That certainly is my name."

" Of Douai ?"

" I reside at Douai."

" Your father's name was Isidore Sarrasin ?"

" It was so."

" Let us conclude him to have been Isidore Sarrasin."

Mr. Sharp drew a note-book from his pocket, consulted it, and resumed—

"Isidore Sarrasin died at Paris in 1857, 6th Arrondissement, Rue Taranne, Number 54—the Hôtel des Écoles, now demolished."

"Perfectly correct," said the doctor, more and more astonished. "But will you have the kindness to explain——?"

"His mother's name," pursued the imperturbable Mr. Sharp, "was Julie Langévol, originally of Bar-le-Duc, daughter of Benedict Langévol, who lived in the alley Loriol, and died in 1812, as is shown by the municipal registers of the said town—these registers are a valuable institution, sir—highly valuable—hem—hem—and sister of Jean Jacques Langévol, drum-major in the 36th Light——"

"I assure you," interrupted Doctor Sarrasin, confounded by this intimate acquaintance with his genealogy, "that you are better informed on these points than I am myself. It is true that my grandmother's family name was Langévol, and that is all I know about her."

"About the year 1807 she left the town of Bar-le-Duc with your grandfather, Jean Sarrasin, whom she had married in 1799. They settled at Melun, where he worked as a tinsmith, and where, in 1811, Julie Langévol, Sarrasin's wife, died, leaving only one child, Isidore

Sarrasin, your father. From that time, up to the date
of his death, discovered at Paris, the thread is lost."

"I can supply it," said the doctor, interested in spite
of himself by this wonderful precision. "My grandfather settled in Paris for the sake of the education of
his son, whom he destined to the medical profession.
He died in 1832, at Palaiseau, near Versailles, where
my father practised as a physician, and where I was born
in 1822."

"You are my man," resumed Mr. Sharp. "No brothers
or sisters ?"

"None. I was the only son; my mother died two
years after my birth. Now, sir, will you tell me—— ?"

Mr. Sharp stood up.

"Rajah Bryah Jowahir Mothooranath," said he, pro-
nouncing the names with the respect shown by every
Englishman to a title, "I am happy to have discovered
you, and to be the first to congratulate you."

"The man is deranged," thought the doctor; "it is not
at all uncommon among these death's heads."

The solicitor read this opinion in his eyes.

"I am not mad in the slightest degree," said he calmly.
"You are at the present moment the sole known heir to
the title of Rajah, which Jean Jacques Langévol—who
became a naturalised British subject in 1819, succeeded to
the property of his wife the Begum Gokool, and died in

1841, leaving only one son, an idiot, who died without issue in 1869—was allowed to assume by the Governor-General of the province of Bengal.

" The value of the estate has risen during the last thirty years to about five millions of pounds sterling. It remained sequestered and under guardianship, almost the whole of the interest going to increase the capital during the life of the imbecile son of Jean Jacques Langévol.

"In 1870 the value of the inheritance was given in round numbers to be twenty-one millions of pounds sterling, or five hundred and twenty-five millions of francs. In fulfilment of an order of the law court of Agra, countersigned by that of Delhi, and confirmed by the Privy Council, the whole of the landed and personal property has been sold, and the sum realised has been placed in the Bank of England.

"The actual sum is five hundred and twenty-seven millions of francs, which you can withdraw by a cheque as soon as you have proved your genealogical identity in the Court of Chancery. And in the meantime I am authorised by Messrs. Trollop, Smith and Co., Bankers, to offer you advances to any amount."

Dr. Sarrasin sat petrified—for some minutes he could not utter a word ; then, impressed by a conviction that this fine story was without any foundation in fact, he quietly said—

"After all, sir, where are the proofs of this, and in what way have you been led to find me out ? "

"The proofs are here, sir," replied Mr. Sharp, tapping on his shiny leather bag. "As to how I discovered you, it has been in a very simple way : I have been searching for you for five years. It is the speciality of our firm to find heirs for the numerous fortunes which year by year are left in escheat in the British dominions.

"For five years the question of the inheritance of the Begum Gokool has exercised all our ingenuity and activity. We have made investigations in every direction, passed in review hundreds of families of your name without finding that of Isidore Sarrasin. I was almost convinced that there was not another of the name in all France, when yesterday morning I read in the *Daily News* a report of the meeting of the Hygienic Conference, and observed that among the members was a Doctor Sarrasin, of whom I had never before heard.

"Referring instantly to my notes, and to hundreds of papers on the subject of this estate, I ascertained with surprise that the town of Douai had entirely escaped our notice.

"With the conviction that I had got on the right scent, took the train for Brighton, saw you leave the meeting, and all doubt vanished. You are the living image of your great-uncle Langévol, of whom we possess a photo-

graph taken from a portrait by the Indian painter
Saranoni."

Mr. Sharp took a photograph from his pocket-book and
handed it to Dr. Sarrasin.

It represented a tall man with a magnificent beard, a
crested turban, and a richly brocaded robe.

He was seated after the manner of conventional portraits
of generals in the army, appearing to be drawing up a plan
of attack, while attentively regarding the spectator.

In the background could be dimly discerned the smoke
of battle and a charge of cavalry.

"A glance at these papers will inform you on this
matter better than I can do," continued Mr. Sharp; "I
will leave them with you, and return in a couple of hours,
if you will then permit me to take your orders."

So saying, Mr. Sharp drew from the depths of his
glazed bag seven or eight bundles of documents, some
printed, some manuscript, placed them on the table, and
backed out of the room, murmuring—

"I have the honour to wish the Rajah Bryah Jowahir
Mothooranath a very good morning."

Partly convinced, partly ridiculing the idea, the doctor
took the papers and began to peruse them.

A rapid examination sufficed to show him the truth
of Mr. Sharp's statements, and to remove his doubts.
Among the printed documents he read the following :

Evidence placed before the Right Honourable Lords of Her Majesty's Privy Council on the 5th of January 1870, touching the vacant succession of the Begum Gokool of Ragginahra, in Bengal. Points of the case. The question concerns the rights of possession to certain landed estates, together with a, variety of edifices, palaces, mercantile establishments, villages, personal properties, treasure, arms, &c., &c., forming the inheritance of the Begum Gokool of Ragginahra.

From evidence submitted to the civil tribunal of Agra, and to the Superior Court at Delhi, it appears that in 1819, the Begum Gokool, widow of Rajah Luckmissur, and possessed in her own right of considerable wealth, married a foreigner, of French origin, by name Jean Jacques Langévol.

This foreigner, after serving until 1815 in [the French army as drum-major in the 36th Light Cavalry, embarked at Nantes, upon the disbandment of the army of the Loire, as supercargo of a merchant ship.

He reached Calcutta, passed into the interior, and speedily obtained the appointment of military instructor in the small native army which the Rajah Luckmissur was authorised to maintain. In this army he rose to be commander-in-chief, and shortly after the Rajah's death he obtained the hand of his widow.

In consideration of various important services rendered

to the English residents at Agra by Jean Jacques Langévol, he was constituted a British subject, and the Governor-General of Bengal obtained for the husband of the Begum the title of Rajah of Bryah Jowahir Mothooranath, which was the name of one of the most considerable of her estates. The Begum died in 1839, leaving the whole of her wealth and property to Langévol, who survived her only two years.

Their only child was imbecile from his infancy, and was placed at once under guardians. The inheritance was carefully managed by trustees until his death, which occurred in 1869.

To this immense heritage there is no known heir. The courts of Agra and Delhi having ordered its sale by auction, on the application of the local government acting for the state, we have the honour to request from the Lords of the Privy Council a confirmation of their decision, &c. Here followed the signatures.

Copies of legal documents from Agra and Delhi, deeds of sale, an account of the efforts made in France to discover the next of kin to Langévol's family, and a whole mass of imposing evidence of the like nature, left Dr. Sarrasin no room for doubt or hesitation.

Between him and the five hundred and twenty-seven millions of francs deposited in the strong rooms of the Bank of England there was but a step, the production of authentic certificates of certain births and deaths.

Such a stroke of fortune being enough to dazzle the imagination of the most sober-minded man, the good doctor could not contemplate it without some emotion. Yet it was of short duration, and exhibited simply by a rapid walk for a few minutes up and down his apartment.

Quickly recovering his self-possession, he accused him-self of weakness for yielding to this feverish agitation, threw himself into his chair, and remained for a time lost in profound reflection.

Then suddenly rising, he resumed his walk backwards and forwards, while his eyes shone with a pure light as though a noble and generous project burned within his breast. He seemed to welcome, to caress, to encourage, and finally to adopt it.

A knock at the door. Mr. Sharp returned.

" I ask pardon a thousand times for my doubts as to the correctness of your information," said the doctor in a cordial tone. " You see me now perfectly convinced, and extremely obliged to you for the trouble you have taken."

" Not at all—mere matter of business—in the way of my profession—nothing more," replied Mr. Sharp. " May I venture to hope that the Rajah will remain our client ? "

" That is understood. I place the whole affair in your hands. I only beg you to desist from giving me that absurd title."

" Absurd !—a title worth twenty millions ! " were the

words Mr. Sharp would have uttered had he known no better; but he said, "Certainly, sir, if you wish it. As you please, sir. I am now going to return by train to London, where I shall await your orders."

"May I keep these documents?" inquired the doctor.

"Most assuredly—we retain copies."

Dr. Sarrasin was left alone. He seated himself at his desk, took out a sheet of paper, and wrote as follows:

"Brighton, 28th October, 1871.

"MY DEAR CHILD,

"We have become possessed of an enormous fortune, a fortune absurdly colossal. Do not fancy that I have lost my senses, but read the printed papers enclosed in my letter. You will there plainly see that I am proved to be the heir to a native title in India, and a sum equivalent to many millions of francs, actually deposited in the Bank of England.

"I can feel sure of the sentiments with which you, my dear Otto, will receive this news. You will perceive, as I do myself, the new duties which such wealth will impose upon us, and the danger we are in of being tempted to use it unwisely.

"It is but an hour since I was made aware of the fact, and already the overpowering sense of responsibility seems to lessen the pleasure it first gave me as I thought of you. This change may be fatal instead of fortunate to our destiny. In the modest position of pioneers of science we were content and happy in obscurity. Shall we continue to be so? I doubt it,—unless—perhaps—(could I venture to mention an idea which has flashed across my brain,) unless this same fortune were to become in our hands a new and powerful engine of science, a mighty tool in the great work of civilisation and progress! We will talk about this. Write to me—let me know very soon what impression this wonderful news makes on your mind—and let your mother hear of it from you. Sensible woman as she is, I am convinced she will receive it calmly. As to your sister, she is too young to have her head turned by anything of the sort. Besides, that little head of hers is a very sober one, and even if she could comprehend all that this change in our position implies, I believe she would take it more quietly than any of us.

"Remember me cordially to Max; I connect him with all my schemes for the future.

"Your affectionate father,

"FRANÇOIS SARRASIN."

This letter, with the more important papers, was addressed to—

Monsieur Octave Sarrasin,

Student at the Upper School of Arts and Manufactures,

32, Rue du Roi de Sicile,

Paris.

Then the doctor put on his overcoat, took his hat, and went to the Conference.

In a quarter of an hour, the worthy man had forgotten all about his millions.

CHAPTER II.

A PAIR OF CHUMS.

DR. SARRASIN'S son Octavius was not exactly what one would call a dunce.   He was neither a blockhead nor a genius, neither plain nor handsome, neither tall nor short, neither dark nor fair.   His complexion was nut-brown, and he was altogether an average specimen of the middle class.

At school he had never taken a very high place, although occasionally gaining a prize.   He had failed in his first examination for passing into the College of Engineers, but a second attempt admitted him, although with no great credit.

There was a want of decision in his character—his mind was content with inaccuracies ; he was one of those people who are satisfied to have a general idea of a subject, and who walk through life by moonlight.

Such men float at the mercy of fate, as corks do on the

crests of waves. They are driven to the equator or to the pole, according to whether the wind blows north or south. Chance decides their career.

Had **Dr.** Sarrasin altogether understood his son's character, he might have hesitated to write the letter he did; but the wisest man may be a blind father.

Fortunately for Octavius, he had during his school life come under the influence of an energetic nature, which by its vigorous strength ruled him for his good, albeit somewhat tyrannically. He formed a close friendship with one of his companions, Max Bruckmann, a native of Alsace, a year younger than himself, but far his superior in physical, intellectual and moral vigour.

Max Bruckmann, left an orphan at the age of twelve, inherited a small income, just sufficient to defray the expense of his education. His life at college would have been monotonous had he not passed the holidays with Octavius, or Otto, as he called his friend, at his home.

The young Alsacien very soon felt himself one of Dr. Sarrasin's family. Beneath a cold exterior lay a warm and sensitive nature, and he considered that he was bound for life to those who acted like father and mother to him.

He positively adored Dr. Sarrasin, his wife, and their pretty thoughtful little daughter; his heart expanded under the influence of their kindness, and he greatly wished to be useful to them by helping Jeannette, who loved her studies, to advance in them, and thoroughly to cultivate her excellent abilities and firm, sensible mind, while he longed to lead Otto to become as good a man as his father. This latter task he well knew to be by no means so easy as the former, yet Max was resolved to attain his double purpose.

Max Bruckmann was one of those trusty and gallant champions whom year by year Alsace sends forth to do battle on the great arena of life in Paris.

As a mere child he distinguished himself by the strength and flexibility of his muscles, as much as by the vivacity and intelligence of his mind. Inwardly full of life and courage, his outward form exhibited strong muscular development rather than graceful proportions. At college he excelled in everything he attempted, whether sport or study. Reaping an annual harvest of prizes, he thought the year wasted if he failed to gain all within his reach.

At twenty his form was large, robust, and in splendid condition; his movements were animated, and his well-shaped head betokened unusual intelligence. When he entered college, the same year with Octavius, he stood second, and was resolved to be first when the time came for leaving it.

Without his persistent energy to urge him forward, Octavius would never have got in at all. For the space of a whole year Max had driven and goaded him to work,

had regularly compelled him to succeed. He entertained
for this friend of weak and vacillating nature a sentiment
of kindly compassion such as one might suppose a lion to
exhibit towards a little puppy. He liked to feel that he
could nourish this parasitical plant from the superabund-
ance of his own sap, and cause it to flourish and blossom
beside him.

The war of 1870 broke out at the close of one of their
terms. Max, full of patriotic grief at the fate which
threatened Strasburg and Alsace, hastened to enlist in the
31st Regiment of Light Infantry. Otto, as Max called
him, and as we will for the future, at once followed his
example.

Side by side the two friends, stationed in the outposts
of Paris, went through the severe campaign of the siege.
At Champigny Max received a ball in his right arm, at
Buzenval an epaulet on his left shoulder. Otto received
neither wound nor decoration. It could not have been his
fault, for he followed his friend everywhere, scarcely half a
dozen yards in his rear. But those half-dozen yards made
all the difference.

After the peace, the two friends resumed their studies,
occupying modest apartments together near the college.

The recent misfortunes of France, the loss to her of
Lorraine and Alsace, had matured the character of Max—
he felt and spoke like a man.

"It is the vocation of the youth of France," said he ; "to repair the errors of their fathers. By genuine hard work alone can this be done."

Max rose every morning at five o'clock, and made Otto do the same. He obliged him to be punctual at his classes, and never lost sight of him during the hours of recreation.

The evening was devoted to study, with occasional pauses for a pipe or a cup of coffee. At ten they retired to rest, their hearts content, their brains well filled.

A game at billiards now and then, a well-chosen play or concert, a ride to the forest of Verrières, a country walk, and twice a week a lesson in fencing and boxing—these were their amusements.

From time to time Otto, casting curious eyes at the very questionable enjoyments of other students, would make feeble attempts at revolt, and talk of going to see Cæsar Leroux, who was "studying law," and passed most of his time at the beer-shop of St. Michel; but Max treated these fancies with such utter contempt and derision that they usually passed off quietly.

On the 29th of October, 1871, about seven o'clock in the evening, the two friends were seated, as was their wont, side by side at the same table, with a shaded lamp between them.

Max was working a problem in applied mathematics,

relative to the stability of blocks, and had thrown himself heart and soul into his subject.

Otto was devoting himself sedulously to something which he thought of much greater consequence, the brewing of a pint of coffee. It was one of the few things in which he flattered himself he really excelled, perhaps because he had daily practice in it, thereby escaping for a few minutes the troublesome business of squaring equations, which he considered that Max really did carry too far.

Drop by drop he let his boiling water pass through a thick layer of powdered mocha, and he ought to have been contented with such tranquil happiness ; but he was annoyed at the devoted industry of Max, and felt an unconquerable desire to interrupt him.

" It would be a good plan to buy a percolator," said he, suddenly. " This ancient and solemn method of filtering is a disgrace to our modern civilisation."

" Do buy a percolator; it will perhaps prevent your wasting an hour every evening with this cookery," replied Max, and he returned to his problem.

" The intrados of a vault is an ellipsoid; let $A\ B\ C\ D$ be that principal ellipse which contains the two axes, $O\ A$ equal to a $O\ B$ equal to b, while the least axis $O\ O'\ C'$ is vertical, and equal to c; then that which supports the elliptic vault———"

At this moment came a rap at the door.

"A letter for Monsieur Octave Sarrasin." It may be imagined that this interruption was heartily welcomed by that young gentleman !

"Ah ! from my father—it is his hand I see. Come, this is something like a letter !" he exclaimed, as he weighed the packet of papers in his hand.

Max knew that the doctor was in England. He had been in Paris a week before on his way there, and had treated the two lads to a dinner fit for an emperor, at the Palais Royal ; for although that once famous place was quite out of fashion, Dr. Sarrasin continued to regard it as the centre of Parisian taste and refinement.

"Let me know what your father says about his Hygienic Conference," said Max. "It was a good idea of his to attend that ; French 'savants' are inclined to be too exclusive."

And Max returned to his problem.

"The extrados will be formed by another similar ellipsoid, having its centre at the point O on the vertical $O\ C$."

"Let $F\ F\ F$ be the foci of the three principal ellipses, then we find the auxiliary ellipse and hyperbola, of which the common axes are——"

A shout from Otto made him look up.

"What is the matter ?" he asked with some alarm, seeing his friend turn pale.

"Read this!" cried Otto, completely astonished by the news he had received.

Max took the letter, read it all through, read it a second time, glanced over the documents enclosed, and said—

"This is curious!"

Then he filled his pipe, and lighted it methodically.

Otto watched him—all anxiety for his opinion.

"Do you think it can be true?" he exclaimed with a choking voice.

"True?—to be sure it is. Your father has too much common sense, his judgment is too good to let him accept rashly so well-authenticated a statement as this. Besides, the proofs are there—it is in fact perfectly plain."

The pipe was now thoroughly lighted.

Max resumed his work.

Otto sat with his arms hanging down, unable even to finish his coffee, far less to bring two ideas together.

He could not help speaking, just to convince himself that he was not asleep.

"But, I say, Max, if this is true it is downright overwhelming! All these millions! why—it is an enormous fortune, mind you!"

Max looked up and nodded, "Yes, enormous is the word for it. Most likely there is not one such in France, a few in the United States, five or six in

England—not above fifteen or twenty in the world altogether."

"And a title into the bargain!" resumed Otto. "A foreign title—what is it? let's see—'Rajah!' Not that I ever was ambitious of having a title, but if it comes in one's way, why it certainly sounds more imposing than plain Sarrasin."

Max shot forth a puff of smoke, and uttered not a word. That puff of smoke distinctly said "Pooh! Pooh!"

"Certainly," continued Otto, "I should never have stuck a 'de' before my name, or assumed anything high-sounding as some people do; but to inherit a real genuine title, and to take rank among the great princes of India, without any possible chance of doubt or confusion!"

The pipe kept puffing "Pooh! Pooh!"

"My dear fellow," said Otto decidedly, "you may say what you like, but I can tell you there is 'a good deal in blood' as the English express it."

He stopped short as he caught the mocking smile in Max's eyes, and returned to the contemplation of his millions.

"Do you recollect, Max, how Binôme, our old arithmetic master, used to impress upon us every year in his opening lesson, that five hundred millions was a number beyond the grasp of one human mind unaided by the resources of written figures? One has to consider that a man spending a franc every minute would take more than a thousand years to pay away such a sum. Well, it really is strange to think one has inherited five hundred millions of francs!"

"Five hundred million francs is it?" cried Max with more interest than he had yet shown. "Shall I tell you the best thing you can do? Give it to France for payment of her ransom, she only requires ten times as much!"

"For mercy's sake, don't suggest such an idea to my father!" cried Otto, looking quite scared. "He really might adopt it. I can tell you that he already has some notion of the kind in his head. Some investment he might certainly make, but at least let us have the interest."

"Come, we shall have you turn out a financier after all!" said Max. "Something tells me, my poor Otto, that it would have been better for your father, with his upright, intelligent mind, if this great fortune had been of a more reasonable size. I would rather see you with an income of five-and-twenty thousand to share with your good little sister than with this great mountain of gold!"

And Max went back to his work.

As to Otto, he could not settle to anything, and fidgeted about the room till his friend got rather impatient and said—

"You had better go out and take a walk, Otto; it is clear you are fit for nothing this evening!"

"You are quite right! I really am not," replied Otto,
who joyfully caught at this excuse for leaving off work,
and seizing his hat, he clattered downstairs, and was soon
in the street.

He presently stopped beneath a bright gaslight, and
read his father's letter again. He wanted to make sure he
was not dreaming.

"Five hundred millions of francs!" he kept repeating.
"That would be at least five-and-twenty millions a year.
Why, if my father will only give me one million a year—
say quarterly or half-yearly—as my allowance, how happy
I should be! Money can do so much. I am sure I should
make an excellent use of it. I'm not a fool—not a bit of
it. Didn't I get into the upper school? And then that
title! I'm sure I could easily support the dignity of a title."

As he passed along he looked into all the shops.

"I shall have a fine house, horses, one for Max of course.
I becoming rich myself, he will become so likewise.
Only think! Five hundred millions! But somehow, now
a fortune comes, it seems to me as though I had expected
it. Something whispered that I should not be poring over
books and plans all my life."

As Otto revolved these thoughts, he was passing along
beneath the arcades of the Rue de Rivoli. Reaching the
Champs Elysées, he turned up the Rue Royal, and
reached the Boulevards.

The splendid shop-fronts, which formerly he regarded with indifference as exhibiting things utterly useless to him, now attracted lively attention, as he considered, with a thrill of delight, that he could at any moment possess any or all of these treasures.

" For me," said he to himself, " for me, all this fine linen, all these exquisite soft cloths are manufactured ; for me watchmakers construct timepieces and chronometers; for my pleasure the brilliant lustres of theatre and opera shed their dazzling light, violins scrape, prima-donnas sing their enchanting strains. For me horse dealers train thorough-breds, and the Café Anglaise is lighted up. All Paris is mine ! Everything is at my disposal ! Travel ! to be sure I shall travel. I shall go and visit my Indian possessions. As likely as not I shall buy a pagoda some day, priests and all, and the ivory idols into the bargain. I shall have elephants of my own ! I shall have splendid guns and rifles—go tiger-shooting. And I must have a beautiful boat. A boat, what am I thinking about ? a fine steam yacht, that's what I shall have—go where I choose, stop as often as I like. Talking of steam, I have to give this news to my mother. Suppose I start for Douai ? There is college to be considered. But then, what's the use of college to me now ? "

" But Max, I must let him know. I should send him a message ; of course he will understand that under present circumstances I am in haste to see my mother and sister."

Otto entered an office, and sent a telegram to inform his friend that he was gone, and would return in a couple of days. Then, hailing a cab, he was driven to the terminus of the Northern Railway.

Settling himself in the corner of a carriage, he continued to follow out his dreaming fancies, until, at two o'clock in the morning, he arrived at Douai; hurried to his father's house, and rang the night bell so noisily, that not only the family, but all the neighbours were aroused by the peal. Night-capped heads popped out at various windows.

" Somebody is very ill !—who can it be ? " inquired one and another.

" The doctor is not at home !" screamed the old servant from her attic window.

" It is I ! it is Otto ! Come down and let me in, Fanchon ! "

After a delay of ten minutes, Otto was admitted into the house. His mother and sister hastily robed in dressing-gowns, came downstairs, all anxiety to learn the cause of this visit.

The doctor's letter on being read aloud explained the mystery.

Madame Sarrasin was at first completely dazzled. She embraced her son and daughter, with tears of joy ; it seemed to her that the whole world was theirs, and that misfortune could never approach a family possessed of hundreds of millions of francs.

Women, however, can more readily than men adapt themselves to circumstances, and to sudden changes of fortune.

Madame Sarrasin read her husband's letter again, felt that this great sum was his, that he would take all the responsibility of deciding what she and her children were to do, and speedily resumed her usual composure.

As to Jeannette, she was glad to see her mother and her brother so happy, but her childish imagination could picture no manner of life more delightful than that she led in her quiet home, occupied with her studies, and happy in the love of her parents.

She could not see why a few bundles of bank-notes should make any such great change in her existence, and the prospect of it did not in the slightest degree discompose her.

Madame Sarrasin had married, at a very early age, a man entirely absorbed by the studious occupations of an ardent scholar and philosopher : she loved her husband, and respected his tastes, although she could not always comprehend them.

Incapable of sharing the pleasure which Dr. Sarrasin derived from study, she had at times felt herself lonely by

the side of the enthusiastic man of science, and consequently centred all her hopes and aspirations in her children. She pictured for them a brilliant and happy future.

Otto, she felt certain, was destined to do great things.
From the time he took a place in the upper school she
mentally regarded that modest and useful college for
young engineers as the nursery of illustrious men. Her
only trouble was that their limited means might possibly
prove an obstacle, or at least a difficulty in the way of her
son's brilliant career, and might ultimately also affect her
daughter's establishment in life. But now, she so far
understood the news conveyed in her husband's letter, as
to perceive that these fears were needless, and her satisfaction was entire.

The mother and son spent most of the night in talking
and making plans, while Jeannette, happy in the present,
heedless of the future, was fast asleep in an arm-chair.

"You have not mentioned Max," said Madame Sarrasin
to her son. "Have you not shown him your father's
letter? What does he say about it?"

"Oh, you know what Max is!" answered Otto. "He is
worse than a philosopher, he is a stoic. I believe he fears
the effect so enormous a fortune will have upon us! I say
upon us, but he is not afraid for my father himself, whose
good sense and judgment, he says, he can rely upon. But
for you, mother, and Jeannette, and more especially for me,

he plainly said he should have preferred an income of a few thousands a year."

"Perhaps Max is not far wrong," replied Madame Sarrasin, looking at her son. "The sudden possession of great wealth is fraught with danger to some natures."

Jeannette awoke, and heard her mother's last words.

"Do not you remember, mother," said she, as, rubbing her eyes, she rose and turned towards her little bedroom, "Do not you remember you told me one day that Max was always in the right. I for my part believe what our friend Max says." And, kissing her mother, Jeannette withdrew.

CHAPTER III.

EFFECT OF AN ITEM OF NEWS.

ON entering the hall, where the fourth meeting of the Hygienic Conference was being held, Dr. Sarrasin was conscious that he was received with unusual tokens of respect. The Right Honourable Lord Glandover, the president and chairman of the assembly, had not hitherto condescended to appear conscious of the existence of the French doctor.

This nobleman was an august personage, whose part it was to declare the Conference open or closed, and, from a list placed before him, to call upon the various speakers who were to address the meeting.

He habitually carried his right hand in the breast of his buttoned coat, not that it had received an injury and needed support, but only because it was usual among English sculptors to represent statesmen in this inconvenient attitude.

His pale smooth face, marked with red blotches, and surmounted by a wig of light hair, brushed high on a forehead which clearly belonged to an empty pate, possessed an aspect of ludicrous stiffness and foolish gravity. Lord Glandover might have been made of wood or paste-board, so stiff and unnatural were all his movements. His very eyes appeared to turn beneath their brows by intermittent jerks, like those of a doll or puppet.

The notice hitherto bestowed on Dr. Sarrasin by Lord Glandover had amounted to no more than a slight and patronising bow; it seemed to say—" Good morning, poor man; you are one of those who support your insignificant existence by making insignificant experiments with insignificant machines. How condescending I am to notice a being so far beneath me in the scale of creation! You may sit down, poor man, beneath the shadow of my nobility."

But on the present occasion Lord Glandover smiled most graciously upon Dr. Sarrasin as he entered, and even carried his courtesy so far as to invite him by a sign to be seated at his right hand. The other members of the Conference all rose when he appeared on the platform.

Considerably astonished by a reception so flattering, Dr. Sarrasin took the chair offered to him, concluding that, on further consideration, his invention had been found of much greater importance than his scientific brethren had

at first supposed.   But this illusion vanished when Lord
Glandover, leaning towards him with a spinal contortion of
his body, whispered in his ear—

"I understand that you are a man of very considerable
property.   They tell me you are worth twenty-one million
pounds sterling."

This was said almost in a tone of reproach, as though his
lordship felt aggrieved at having lightly treated the equivalent in flesh and blood of a sum of money so vast.

His look and tone seemed to say—

"Why was I not made aware of this?   It really is very
unfair to expose one to the awkwardness of making such
mistakes!"

Dr. Sarrasin, who could not in conscience have said he
"was worth" a penny more than he had been at the last
meeting, was wondering how the news should have already
become known, when Dr. Ovidius of Berlin, who sat next
him, said with a false and faint smile—

"Why, Sarrasin, you are as great a man as any of the
Rothschilds!—so the *Daily Telegraph* makes out.   Let me
congratulate you."

He handed the doctor a copy of the paper of Thursday.
Among the items of news was to be seen the following
paragraph, the composition of which plainly revealed its
authorship.

"A MONSTER HERITAGE.—The legitimate heir to the

fortune of the late Begum Gokool has at length been dis-
covered, thanks to the indefatigable researches of Messrs.
Billows, Green and Sharp, solicitors, 94, Southampton
Row, London.

"The fortunate possessor of twenty-one million pounds
sterling, now deposited in the Bank of England, is a
Frenchman, Dr. Sarrasin, whose able paper, communicated
at the Brighton Scientific Conference, was reported in this
journal three days ago.

"By dint of a course of strenuous efforts, and amid
difficulties and adventures forming in themselves a perfect
romance, Mr. Sharp has succeeded in proving indisputably
that Dr. Sarrasin is the sole living descendant of Jean
Jacques Langévol, the second husband of the Begum
Gokool.

" This soldier of fortune was, it appears, a native of the
town of Bar-le-Duc in France.

" A few matters of form only required to be gone through
in order to place Dr. Sarrasin in full possession of his fortune.   A petition to that effect has been filed in Chancery.

"Very remarkable is the chain of circumstance by which
the treasure accumulated by a long line of Indian Rajahs
is laid at the feet of a French physician. The fickle
goddess might have exhibited the indiscretion she so
frequently displays in the disposal of her gifts ; but on
this occasion she has, we are glad to say, bestowed this

prodigious fortune on one who will not fail to make a good use of his wealth."

Oddly enough, as many might think, Dr. Sarrasin was vexed to see his news made public. He not only foresaw the many annoyances it would entail upon him, he also felt humbled by the importance people seemed to attach to the event. He, himself personally, appeared to dwindle into insignificance before the imposing figures which denoted his capital. He was inly conscious that his own personal merits, and all he had ever accomplished, were already, even in the eyes of those who knew him best, sunk in this ocean of gold and silver.

His friends no longer saw in him the enthusiastic experimentalist, the ingenious inventor, the acute philosopher ; they saw only the great millionaire.

Had he been a hump-backed dwarf, an ignorant Hottentot, the lowest specimen of humanity, instead of one of its most intelligent representatives, his value would have been the same as Lord Glandover had expressed it, he "was worth" henceforth just twenty-one million pounds, no more and no less.

This idea sickened him, and the crowd of members, staring with a searching if not a scientific curiosity to see how a millionaire looked, remarked with surprise that a shade of melancholy gathered on the countenance under examination.

This, however, was only a passing weakness.

The magnitude of the object to which he had resolved to dedicate his unexpected fortune rose suddenly before him, and his serenity was restored.

He waited until Dr. Stevenson, of Glasgow, had finished reading a paper on the education of young idiots, and then requested leave to make a communication.

It was instantly granted by Lord Glandover, although the name of Dr. Ovidius stood next on the list. By the marked tone of his voice, he indicated that he would have done so had the whole Conference objected, or had all the learned men in Europe protested with one accord against such a piece of favouritism.

"Gentlemen," said Dr. Sarrasin, "it was my intention to wait for a few days before informing you of the singular chance which has befallen me, and of the happy consequences which may result to science from this event. But, the fact having become public, it would seem mere affectation were I now to delay speaking of it, and placing it in its proper light.

"Yes, gentlemen, it is true that a large sum of money, a sum amounting to many millions, now deposited in the Bank of England, appears to be legally my property.

"Need I tell you, that such being the case, I consider myself simply as a steward, entrusted with this wealth for the use and benefit of science? (Immense sensation.) This treasure belongs, not to me but to humanity—to

progress ! (Great commotion—exclamations—applause.
The whole assembly, electrified by this announcement,
rise *en masse.*)

" Do not applaud me, gentlemen ; I know not one man of
science worthy of the name who, in my place, would not
do what it is my desire to do.

" It is possible that some may attribute to me motives of
vanity and self-love in this matter, rather than of genuine
devotedness. (No ! No !) It matters little. Let us look
to the results.

" I declare, then, definitively, and without reservation,
that the twenty-one million pounds placed in my hands
belongs not to me, but to science ! Will you, gentlemen,
undertake the management and distribution of it ?

" I have not sufficient confidence in my own knowledge to
undertake the sole disposal of such a sum. I appoint you
as trustees ; you yourselves shall decide on the best means
of employing all the treasure." (Tumultuous applause—
great excitement—general enthusiasm.)

The whole assembly stood up, some members, in the
fever of excitement, mounted on the table. Professor
Turnbull, of Glasgow, appeared on the verge of apoplexy.
Dr. Cicogna, of Naples, was ready to choke.

Lord Glandover alone maintained the serene and dig‐
nified composure befitting his rank. He was perfectly
convinced that Dr. Sarrasin intended the whole thing as a

pleasant jest, without the smallest intention of actually carrying out so extravagant a scheme.

When quiet was in some measure restored, the speaker continued—

"If I may be permitted to suggest what it would be easy to develop and bring to perfection, I would beg to propose the following plan."

The assembly, recovering its composure, listened with reverential attention.

"Gentlemen, among the many causes of the sickness, misery and death which surround us, is one to which I think it reasonable to attach great importance; and that is the deplorable sanitary conditions under which the greater part of mankind exists.

"Multitudes are massed together in towns, and in dwellings where they are often deprived of light and air, the two elements most necessary to life.

"These agglomerations of humanity become the hotbeds of fever and infection, and even those who escape death are tainted with disease; they are feeble and useless members of society, which thereby suffers great and serious loss, instead of deriving priceless advantage from their healthful and vigorous labour.

"Why, gentlemen, should we not, in an effort to remedy this sore evil, try the most powerful of all means of persuasion—that of example?

"Why should we not, by uniting the powers of our minds, produce the plan of a model city, based upon strictly scientific principles? (Cries of Hear, Hear.) Why should we not afterwards devote our capital to the erection of such a city, and then present it to the world as a practical illustration of what all cities ought to be?" (Hear, Hear! and thunders of applause.)

The members, in transports of admiration, shook hands, and congratulated each other; then, surrounding Dr. Sarrasin, they seized upon his chair, raised him up, and bore him triumphantly round the hall.

"Gentlemen," continued the doctor, on being permitted to resume his place; "to this city, which every one of us can already picture in imagination, and which may shortly become a reality—to this city of health and happiness we will call universal attention by descriptions, translated into all the languages of the earth; we will invite visitors from every nation; we will offer it as a home and refuge for honest families forced to emigrate from over-populated countries.

"Those unfortunate people, also, who are driven into exile by foreign conquest (can you wonder, gentlemen, that I think of them?) will find with us employment for their activity, and scope for their intelligence, while they will enrich our colony by their moral virtue and intellectual strength—possessions of far higher value than gold or precious stones.

" We will found great colleges where youth will be trained and educated in principles based on the truest wisdom, so as to develop and justly balance their moral, physical, and intellectual faculties, thus preparing future generations of strong and virtuous men."

No language can describe the tumult of enthusiasm which followed this communication. For at least a quarter of an hour the hall resounded with a storm of cheering and hurrahs.

Dr. Sarrasin sat down, and Lord Glandover, once more leaning towards him, murmured in his ear with a knowing wink—

"Not a bad speculation that! what a revenue you would draw from the tolls—eh ? The thing would be sure to succeed, provided it were well started and backed up by influential names. Why, all our convalescents and valetu- dinarians would be for settling there at once! Be sure you put down my name for a good building lot, doctor !"

Poor Dr. Sarrasin was quite mortified by this determina- tion to attribute his actions to a covetous motive, and was about to reply to his lordship, when he heard the vice- president move a vote of thanks to the author of the philanthropic proposal just submitted to the assembly.

" It would," he said, " be to the eternal honour of the

Brighton Conference, that an idea so sublime had been
originated there. It was an idea which nothing short of
the most exalted benevolence and the rarest generosity
could have conceived. And yet, now that the idea had
been suggested, it seemed almost a wonder that it had
never before occurred to any one.

"Millions had been lavished on senseless wars, vast
capitals squandered in foolish speculations ; how infinitely
better spent they might have been in the furtherance of
such a scheme as this ! "

The speaker, in conclusion, proposed " That, in honour
of its founder, the new city should receive the name of
Sarrasina."

This motion would have been carried by acclamation,
but Dr. Sarrasin interposed—

" No," said he, " my name has nothing whatever to do
with this scheme.   Neither let us bestow on the future
city a fancy name derived from Greek or Latin, such as
is often invented, and gives an air of affectation and
peculiarity to whatever bears it. It will be the city of
welfare and comfort, let it be named after my country.
Let us call it Frankville ! "

Every one agreed to gratify Dr. Sarrasin in this by
acceding to his choice, and the first step was thus taken
towards the founding of the city.

The meeting then proceeded to the discussion of other

points, and to this practical occupation, so unlike those to which it was usually devoted, we will leave it, while we follow the wandering fortunes of the paragraph published in the *Daily Telegraph.*

Copied word for word by all the newspapers, the information contained in this little paragraph was soon blazed abroad, over every county in England. In the *Hull Gazette* it figured at the top of the second page in a copy of that modest journal which, on the first of November, arrived at Rotterdam on board the three-masted collier *Queen Mary.*

The active scissors of the editor of the *Belgian Echo* pounced upon it at once, it was speedily translated into Flemish (the language of Cuyp and Potter), and on the wings of steam it reached the *Bremen Chronicle* on the 2nd of November. In that paper our bit of news next appeared, the same in substance, but clothed in a garb of German, the artful editor adding in parenthesis "from our Brighton correspondent."

The anecdote, now thoroughly Germanised, reached the office of the editor of the *Northern Gazette*, and that great man gave it a place in the second column of his third page.

On the evening of the 3rd of November, after passing through these various transformations, it made its entrance, between the fat hands of a stout serving man, into the study of Professor Schultz of the University of Jena.

High as this personage stood in the scale of humanity, he presented nothing remarkable to the eye of a stranger.

He was a man of five or six and forty, strongly built, his square shoulders denoting a robust constitution; his forehead was bald, the little hair remaining on his temples and behind his head suggested the idea that they consisted of threads of tow. His eyes were blue, that vague blue which never betrays a thought. Professor Schultz had a large mouth, garnished with a double row of formidable teeth which would never drop their prey; thin lips closed over them, whose principal employment was to keep note of the words which passed between them.

The general appearance of the professor was decidedly unpleasant to others, but he himself was evidently perfectly satisfied with it.

On hearing his servant enter, he raised his eyes to a very pretty clock over the mantel-piece which looked out of place among a number of vulgar articles around it, and said in a quick, rough voice—

"6.55! The post comes in at 6.30. You bring my letters too late by twenty-five minutes. The next time they are not on my table at 6.30 you quit my service."

"Will you please to dine now, sir?" asked the man as he withdrew.

"It is now 6.55, and I dine at seven. You have been

here for three weeks, and you know that. Recollect that I never change an hour, and never repeat an order."

The professor laid his newspaper on the table, and went on writing a treatise which was to appear next day in 'Physiological Records,' a periodical to which he contributed. We may be permitted to state that this treatise was entitled—" *Why are all Frenchmen affected by different degrees of hereditary degeneracy ?* "

As the professor pursued his task, his dinner, consisting of a large dish of sausages and cabbage, flanked by a huge flagon of beer, was carefully placed on a round table near the fire.

He laid aside his pen in order to partake of this repast, which he did with greater appearance of enjoyment than might have been expected from so grave an individual. Then he rang for coffee, lighted his pipe, and resumed his labours.

It was after midnight when he signed his name on the last page, and retired at once to his bedroom to enjoy a well-earned repose.

Not till he was in bed did he take his paper from its cover, and begin to read before going to sleep. Just as the professor was becoming drowsy, his eye was caught by a foreign name, that of "Langévol," in the paragraph relating to the "Monster Heritage." He tried to call to mind clearly the vague recollections to which this name

gave rise. After a few minutes vainly devoted to efforts
of memory, he threw away the journal, blew out his candle,
and loud snores quickly gave notice that he slept.

By a physiological phenomenon, which he himself had
studied and explained at great length, this name of
Langévol followed Professor Schultz even in his dreams.
The consequence was that on awaking next morning, he
found himself mechanically repeating it.

All at once, just as he was going to look at his watch, a
sudden light broke upon him.

Snatching up the newspaper at the foot of his bed, he
read again and again, with his hand pressed on his forehead,
the paragraph which he had all but missed seeing the night
before. The light was evidently spreading to his brain,
for without waiting to put on his flowered dressing-gown,
he hurried to the fireplace, took a small miniature portrait
from the wall by the mirror, and turning it round, passed
his sleeve across the dusty pasteboard at the back.

The professor was right. Behind the picture he read
the following German words, traced in faded ink :

" Therese Schultz, eine geborene Langévol," which means,
" Theresa Schultz, whose maiden name was Langévol."

That evening the professor was in the express train on
his way to London.

CHAPTER IV.

TWO CLAIMANTS.

ON the 6th November, at 7 A.M., Professor Schultz arrived at the Charing Cross Station. At noon he presented himself at No 94, Southampton Row, entering a large room divided by a wooden barrier, one side being for the clerks, the other for the public. In it there were six chairs, a table, numberless green tin boxes, and a London Directory. Two young men, seated at the table, were quietly eating the traditional luncheon of bread and cheese usual with their class.

" Messrs. Billows, Green, and Sharp ?" said the professor, in the tone of a man calling for his dinner.

" Mr. Sharp is in his private room—what name ? On what business ?"

" Professor Schultz, of Jena. On the Langévol business."

This information was murmured into the speaking-tube by the young clerk; a reply being returned into his ear which he did not choose to repeat—

" Hang the Langévol business ! Another fool come to put in a claim !"

Clerk's answer—

" This man seems respectable enough. Does not look exactly agreeable though."

Another mysterious whisper conveyed the words—

" And he comes from Germany."

" So he says."

With a sigh came the order—

" Send him upstairs."

" Second story, door facing you," said the clerk aloud, pointing to an inner entrance.

The professor plunged into the passage, mounted the stairs, and found himself opposite a green baize door, on which the name of **Mr. Sharp** stood out in black letters on a brass plate.

That personage was seated at a large mahogany writing-table, in a common-looking room, with a felt carpet, leather chairs, and many open boxes.

He half rose from his seat, and then, according to **the** polite fashion of business men, began to rummage amongst his papers for several minutes to show how busy he was. At last, turning to Professor Schultz who remained standing near him, he said—

" Have the goodness, sir, to tell me your business here in as few words as possible. My time is limited ; I can give you but a very few minutes."

The professor smiled slightly, evidently not at all put out by the way he was received.

"Perhaps," he said, "when you know what brings me here, you will think it advisable to grant me a few minutes more."

"Proceed, sir."

"My business relates to the inheritance left by Jean Jacques Langévol, of Bar-le-Duc. I am the grandson of the elder sister, Theresa Langévol, who married in 1792 my grandfather, Martin Schultz, a surgeon in the army of Brunswick; he died in 1814. I have in my possession three letters from my great-uncle, written to his sister, and many accounts of his return home after the battle of Jena, besides the legal documents which prove my birth."

We need not follow Professor Schultz through the prolix explanations which he gave to Mr. Sharp. On this point he seemed, contrary to his nature, quite inexhaustible. His aim was to demonstrate to this Englishman, this Mr. Sharp, that by rights the German race should, in all things, predominate over all others. His object in putting forward a claim to this inheritance was chiefly that it might be snatched from French hands, which could not fail to make a silly use of it. What he hated in his rival was his nationality. Had he been a German he certainly should not have interfered, &c., &c.

But that a Frenchman—a would-be "savant"—should

have this enormous wealth to spend upon French fancies, was distracting to his feelings, and he considered it his duty to contest his right to it at all costs.

At first sight, the connection between these political opinions and the opulent inheritance in question was not very clear. But the experienced eye of the man of business plainly detected the relation which patriotic ambition for the advantage of the German nation generally, bore to the private interests of Professor Schultz individually. He saw that this apparently double aim had in reality but one motive.

There was no doubt about it. However humiliating it might be for a professor of the University of Jena to be connected with beings of an inferior race, it was evident that a French ancestress had had a share in the responsibility of giving to the world this matchless human being.

But this relationship being in a secondary degree to that of Doctor Sarrasin, would only give secondary rights to the said inheritance. The solicitor perceived, however, the possibility of lawfully sustaining them, and in this possibility he foresaw another which would be much to the advantage of Billows, Green, and Sharp, something which would change the Langévol affair, already productive, into a very good thing, indeed, a second case of the "Jarndyce *versus* Jarndyce" of Dickens. An extensive horizon of stamped paper, deeds, documents of all sorts, rose before the eyes of the man of law; and, what was worth more, he saw a compromise conducted by himself, Sharp, to the interest of both his clients, which would bring to himself equal parts of honour and profit.

In the meanwhile he made known to Professor Schultz the claims of Doctor Sarrasin, gave him proofs in corroboration, and insinuated that if Billows, Green, and Sharp undertook to make something advantageous for the professor out of the claims, "shadowy though they are, my dear sir, it would, I fear, not hold water in a lawsuit," which his relationship to the doctor gave him—he hoped that the remarkable sense of justice, possessed by all Germans, would admit that to Messrs. Billows, Green, and Sharp, he, the professor, owed a large debt of gratitude.

The latter was practical enough to understand the drift of this argument, and soon put the mind of the business man at rest on this point, though without committing himself in any way. Mr. Sharp politely begged permission to examine into the affair at his leisure, showed him out with marked respect, nothing more having been said as to the very limited time of which before he had been so sparing.

Professor Schultz retired convinced that he had no sufficient claim to put forward for the Begum's inheritance, but all the same persuaded that a struggle between the Saxon and Latin races, besides being always meritorious, would not fail, if set about properly, to turn to the advantage of the former.

The next important step was to get Dr. Sarrasin's opinion on the subject. A telegram despatched immediately to Brighton had the effect of bringing that gentleman to Mr. Sharp's office by five o'clock.

Dr. Sarrasin heard all that had occurred with a calmness which astonished the solicitor. He frankly declared that he perfectly remembered a tradition in his family of a great-aunt brought up by a rich and titled lady, who had emigrated with her, and who had married in Germany. He knew neither the name nor the exact degree of relationship of this great-aunt.

Mr. Sharp was busily looking over his notes, carefully numbered in portfolios, which he now exhibited with considerable complacency to the doctor.

There was—Mr. Sharp did not seek to hide it—mattei for a lawsuit, and lawsuits of this character may easily be lengthened out. Indeed, it was not at all necessary to acknowledge to the adverse party that family tradition which Doctor Sarrasin had in his honesty just now confided to his solicitor. To be sure, there were those letters from Jean Jacques Langévol to his sister, of which Professor Schultz had spoken, and which were a point in his favour. A very small point indeed, destitute of any legal character, but still a point—no doubt other proofs would be exhumed from the dust of municipal archives. Perhaps even the adverse party, in default of authentic documents, would even dare to manufacture false ones. Everything must be foreseen. Who knew but that fresh investigations might assign to this Thérèse Langévol and her descendants, who had suddenly started up, superior claims to Dr. Sarrasin's ? In any case, there would be long disputes, tedious examinations—no end of them. There was good hope of success for both sides, each could easily form a limited liability company to advance the cost of the proceedings and exhaust all the pleas of jurisdiction.

A celebrated suit of the same sort had been in the Court of Chancery for eighty-three consecutive years, and was only ended at last for want of funds—interest and capital, all had gone ! What with inquiries, commissions, transfers, the proceedings would take an indefinite period ! In ten years' time the question would probably be still undecided, and the twenty-one millions still sleeping quietly in the Bank.

Dr. Sarrasin listened to this long-winded oration, and wondered when it would come to an end. Without taking for gospel all that he heard, he felt a kind of chilly discouragement creeping over him, as a voyager gazes from the ship's bows at the port to which he believes himself approaching, but sees it growing less and less distinct, and finally disappearing as his vessel drifts away from the

land. He told himself that it was not impossible that this
fortune just now so near, and for which he had already
found a use, would end by slipping from his grasp, and
fade away.

"Then what is to be done ?" he asked of the solicitor.

"What is to be done ?—Hem!—That was difficult to
say, more difficult still to decide ; but no doubt everything
would be arranged in the end. He, Sharp, was certain of
that. English law was excellent, a leetle slow perhaps,
he could not help saying so—yes, decidedly slow, *pede
claudo*—hem !—hem !—but all the more sure. Assuredly
Doctor Sarrasin could not fail in the course of a few years
to be in possession of this inheritance, always supposing—
hem !—hem !—his claims sufficient ! "

The doctor issued from the office in Southampton Row
very much shaken in his confidence, and convinced that he
must either plunge into an interminable lawsuit or give
up his dream. The thoughts that his fine philanthropic
scheme must come to nothing gave him keen pain.

In the meantime, Mr. Sharp sent for Professor Schultz,
who had left his address. He told him that Dr. Sarrasin
had never heard of Thérèse Langévol, denied the existence
of a German branch of the family, and rejected any idea of
a compromise. There was nothing that the professor could
do, therefore, if he believed his right well established, but to
go to law. From this, Mr. Sharp, who was perfectly dis-

interested of course, and was a mere spectator in the matter, had no intention of dissuading him. What more could a solicitor wish than a lawsuit of perhaps thirty years, and not knowing to what it might lead them. He personally would be delighted. If he had not feared that Professor Schultz would think it suspicious on his part; he would have pushed his disinterestedness so far as to recommend to him one of his legal brethren, who would look after his interests. And, indeed, the choice was an important one! The path of law had now become a regular high road!—swarming with adventurers and robbers!—he owned this shameful fact, though with a blush!

"Supposing the French doctor was willing to arrange the matter, how much would it cost?" asked the professor.

Being a wise man, words could not confuse him—being a practical man, he went straight to the point without wasting any precious time on the way. Mr. Sharp was rather disconcerted by this mode of action. He represented to Professor Schultz that business did not go on so quickly as all that; that no one could see the end, when as yet they were just at the beginning; that in order to bring Dr. Sarrasin to terms they must protract the business, so as not to allow him to see that he, Schultz, was at all eager to compromise matters.

"I beg, sir," he concluded, "that you will leave it to me;

put yourself in my hands, and I will be answerable for everything."

"Very well," replied Schultz, "but I should much like to know what I have to expect."

However, he could not ascertain from Mr. Sharp the price at which the solicitor valued Saxon gratitude, and was therefore obliged to give him *carte blanche* in the matter.

When Dr. Sarrasin appeared next day in answer to Mr. Sharp's summons, and quietly asked if he had any particular news for him, the solicitor, alarmed at his calmness, informed him that a serious examination had convinced him that the better plan would be to nip the threatened danger in the bud, and propose to compromise with this new claimant. Dr. Sarrasin must agree with him that this was essentially disinterested advice, and what few solicitors in Mr. Sharp's place would have given. But he felt quite a paternal interest in the affair, and his pride was concerned in bringing it to a speedy conclusion.

The doctor listened and thought all this sensible enough. During the last few days he had become so accustomed to the idea of immediately realising his scientific dream that everything gave way to it. To wait ten years, or even one year before he had it in his power, would have been a cruel trial to him. Without being taken in by Mr. Sharp's fine speeches, although little familiar with legal and financial questions, he would have cheerfully given up his claims for a sum paid down in ready money sufficient to enable him to pass at once from theory to practice. He also, therefore, at once, gave *carte blanche* to Mr. Sharp, and departed.

The solicitor had now got what he wanted. It was quite true that perhaps another might in his place have yielded to the temptation of beginning and prolonging a lawsuit which would bring in a considerable annuity to his business. But Mr. Sharp was not a man who cared for this kind of speculation.

He saw close to his hand a way by which he could reap an abundant harvest, and he resolved to seize it. The next day he wrote to the doctor that he believed Herr Schultz was not opposed to a compromise. In subsequent visits made by him to the doctor and professor, he told them alternately, that the adverse party would say nothing decided, and that, in addition, a third candidate, attracted by the scent, was talked of.

This little game went on for a week. In the morning all was going well, but by the evening an unforeseen objection had suddenly arisen to upset everything. The honest doctor was incessantly troubled by doubts, fears, and changes of mind. Mr. Sharp could not bring himself to hook his fish, he so greatly feared that at the last he would struggle and snap the line. But so many precautions were, in this case, quite superfluous. From the very first day Dr. Sarrasin,

who would have done anything to spare himself the trouble
of a lawsuit, was ready for any arrangement. When at
last Mr. Sharp thought that the psychological moment, to
use the celebrated expression, had arrived, or in less exalted
language, that his client was done to a turn, he suddenly
unmasked his batteries, and proposed an immediate compromise.

A benevolent man then appeared—the banker, Stilbing—
who proposed to split the difference, to give to each ten
millions, and merely have for commission the surplus
million.

Dr. Sarrasin could have embraced Mr. Sharp when he
made him this proposal; it seemed splendid to him.
He was ready and eager to sign. He would have
liked to put up in the market place of the proposed
city golden statues to the banker Stilbing, to the solicitor
Sharp, to the bank and to all the lawyers in the United
Kingdom.

The documents were drawn up, and everything was
ready. Professor Schultz had surrendered—Mr. Sharp
assuring him that, with a less easy-tempered adversary he
would certainly have had all costs to pay. So it was
settled. The two heirs each received a cheque for a
hundred thousand pounds, payable at sight, and a promise
of a definite settlement after all the legal formalities had
been gone through.

Thus was this wonderful affair settled, to the great glory of the Anglo-Saxon race!

We are assured that, that same evening, whilst dining at the Cobden Club with his friend Stilbing, Mr. Sharp drank a glass of champagne to the health of Dr. Sarrasin, another to Professor Schultz, and then, as he finished the bottle, gave way to this somewhat indiscreet exclamation—

"Hurrah! Rule Britannia! We've got the best of it this time!"

The truth is, that the banker Stilbing considered his friend rather stupid for not having made a great deal more out of the business, and in his heart the professor had thought the same, from the moment in which he had felt himself obliged to agree to any arrangement that was offered. What could not have been done with a man like Dr. Sarrasin, a Celt, careless, thoughtless, and very certainly visionary!

The professor had heard of his rival's project of founding a French town, under such moral and physical conditions as would develop the qualities of the race, and form strong and brave generations.

This enterprise appeared to him absurd, and, to his ideas, sure to fail, as it opposed the law of progress, which decreed the uprooting of the Latin race, its subjection to the Saxon, and eventually its disappearance from the surface of the globe. However, these results might be held in check if

the doctor's programme began to be realised, and so much
the more if there was any prospect of its success. It was,
therefore, the duty of every true Saxon, in the interest of
general order, to obey this appointed law, and bring to
nothing, if he could, this insane enterprise. Under the
circumstances it was quite clear that he, Schultz, M.D.,
privat docent of chemistry in Jena University, known by
his numerous works on the different human races,—works
in which it was proved that the German race was to absorb
all others—it was quite clear that he was particularly
designed by the great creative and destructive force of
nature to annihilate the pigmies who were struggling against
it. From the very beginning it had been ordained that
Thérèse Langévol would marry Martin Schultz, and that
one day, the two nationalities meeting in the persons of
the French doctor and the German professor, the latter
would crush the former. Already he had in his possession
half the doctor's fortune,—this was the weapon he was to
wield.

This project was but a secondary one to Professor
Schultz at present ; he merely added it to others still
more vast which he had formed for the destruction of all
nations who refused to blend themselves with the German
people and be united with the Vaterland. However, wishing
to explore to the end—if so be that they had an end—of
Dr. Sarrasin's plans, he attended all the meetings of the

Congress. As several members, with Doctor Sarrasin himself among them, were leaving the meeting, the professor was overheard to make this declaration : that he would found at the same time as Frankville, a city strong enough to put an end to that absurd and abnormal ant-hill.

" I hope," he added, " that the experiment we shall make will serve as an example to all the world !"

Although good Doctor Sarrasin was so full of love to all mankind, he had lived long enough to know that all his fellow-creatures did not deserve the name of philanthropists. He noted, however, this speech of his adversary, thinking like a sensible man that no threat ought to be neglected. Some time afterwards, writing to Max to invite him to aid in his enterprise, he mentioned this incident and described Herr Schultz so accurately that the young Alsacian was certain the doctor had in him a formidable adversary. The doctor added—

" We shall need bold and energetic men, of practical information, not only to build, but to defend us."

Max answered—

" Although I cannot immediately give my co-operation to the founding of your city, you may depend on finding me when the right time comes. I shall not lose sight for a single day of this Professor Schultz whom you have described so well. My Alsacian birth gives me the right to know about his affairs. Whether I am near you or far

away, I am devoted to you.   If by any unforeseen chance
you should be some months, or even years, without hearing
from me, do not be uneasy.   Whether I am near you or
far away, I shall have but one thought, to work for you,
and consequently to serve France."

CHAPTER V.

STAHLSTADT.

WE must take a leap through time and space. Five years have elapsed since the two heirs took possession of the Begum's inheritance. The scene lies in the United States, to the south of Oregon, ten leagues from the shores of the Pacific. The district is mountainous, its northern limits as yet barely defined by the two neighbouring powers.

A merely superficial spectator might call it the American Switzerland, with its abrupt peaks rising above the clouds, its deep valleys dividing the heights, its aspect at once grand and wild.

But, unlike the European Switzerland, it is not given up to the peaceful industries of the shepherd, the guide, and the hotel-keeper. It has Alpine decorations only, just a crust of rocks, and earth and venerable pines spread over a mass of iron and coal.

Should the traveller through these solitudes stay on his
way to listen awhile to the voice of nature, he would not,
as on the slopes of the Oberland, hear the gentle murmurs
of insect life, or the herd-boy's call, enhancing the silence
of the mountain. On his ear in this wild spot would fall
the heavy sound of the steam hammer, and under his feet
would echo the muffled explosions of powder.

He would feel as if the ground was as full of trap-doors
as the stage of a theatre, and that at any moment even the
huge rocks might sink and disappear into unknown depths.

Dreary roads, black with cinders and coke, wind round
the sides of the mountains.

Heaps of variegated scoria, which the scanty herbage
fails to cover, glance and glare like the eyes of a basilisk.
Here and there yawns the shaft of a deserted mine, a dark
gulf, the mouth grown over with briers. The air is heavy
with smoke, and hangs like a pall over the ground. Not
a bird nor an insect is to be found, and a butterfly has not
been seen within the memory of man.

At the northern point, where the mountain-spurs slope
into the plain, lies between two ranges of bleak hills what
up to 1871 was called the "red plain," because of the
colour of the soil, which is impregnated with oxide of
iron, but what is now called Stahlfeld, or the field of
steel.

Just imagine a plateau of seventeen or eighteen square

STAHLSTADT.   [*Page* 65.

miles, the soil sandy and strewn with pebbles, and altogether as arid and desolate as the ancient bed of some inland sea. Nature has done nothing towards giving life and movement to the place, but man has brought a wonderful amount of energy and vigour to bear on it.

In five years there sprang up on this bare and rocky plain eighteen villages, composed of small wooden houses, all alike, brought ready built from Chicago, and containing a large population of rough workmen.

In the midst of these villages, at the very foot of the Coal Butts, as the inexhaustible mountains of coal are called, rises a dark mass, huge, and strange, an agglomeration of regular buildings, pierced with symmetrical windows, covered with red roofs, and surmounted by a forest of cylindrical chimneys, which continually vomit forth clouds of dense smoke. Through the black curtain which veils the sky, dart red lightning-like flames, while a distant roaring is heard resembling that of thunder or the beating of the surf on a rocky shore.

This erection is Stahlstadt—Steel Town! The German city, and the personal property of Professor Schultz, the ex-chemistry professor of Jena, who has become, by means of the Begum's millions, the greatest iron-worker, and especially the greatest cannon-founder, of the two hemispheres.

He casts guns of all shapes and of all calibres, smooth

and rifled bores, for Russia, Turkey, Roumania, Japan, foɪ
Italy and for China, but particularly for Germany.

With the aid of his enormous capital, this large establishment, which is at the same time a regular town, started up
as at the wave of a conjurer's wand. Thirty thousand
workmen, Germans for the most part, crowded to it, and
settled themselves in the suburbs. In a few months its
products, owing to their overwhelming superiority, acquired
universal celebrity.

Professor Schultz digs out iron and coal from his own
mines, which lie ready to his hand, changes them into
steel, and again into cannon, all on the spot.

What none of his competitors can do he manages. In
France ingots of steel are obtained, eighty thousand pounds
in weight. In England a hundred-ton gun has been cast.
At Essen M. Krupp has contrived to cast blocks of steel
of ten hundred thousand pounds! Herr Schultz does not
stop at that—he knows no limits. Order a cannon of him,
of whatever weight and power you like, he'll turn you out
that cannon, as bright as a new halfpenny, exactly at the
time agreed on.

But he makes his customers pay for it! It is as if the
two hundred and fifty millions of 1871 had only given him
an appetite for more!

In gun-casting, as in everything else, the man who can
do what others cannot is sure to be well off. Indeed,

Schultz's cannon not only attain to an unprecedented size, but, although they may deteriorate slightly by use, they never burst. Stahlstadt steel seems to have special properties. There are many stories current of mysterious chemical mixtures; but one thing is certain, that no one has discovered the invaluable secret.

Another thing certain is that, in Stahlstadt, that secret is guarded with the most jealous care.

In this remote corner of North America, surrounded by deserts, isolated from the world by a rampart of mountains, five hundred miles from the nearest town or habitation of any sort, we may search in vain for the smallest vestige of that liberty which is the foundation principle of the United States.

On arriving under the walls of Stahlstadt it is useless to try and enter one of the massive gateways which here and there break the line of moats and fortifications. The sternest of sentinels will repulse the traveller. He must go back to the suburbs. He cannot enter the City of Steel unless he possesses the magic formula, the password, or, at any rate, an order, duly stamped, signed, and countersigned.

One November morning a young workman arrived at Stahlstadt, who doubtlessly possessed such an order, for after leaving his well-worn portmanteau at an inn, he directed his steps to the gateway nearest the village.

He was a fine, strongly built young fellow, dressed in a loose coat, woollen shirt, with no collar, and trousers of ribbed velveteen, tucked into big boots. He pulled his wide felt hat over his eyes, as if to conceal the coal dust with which his skin was begrimed, and walked forward with elastic step, whistling through his brown moustache.

Arrived at the gateway, the young man, showing a printed paper to the officer of the gate, was immediately admitted.

"Your order is addressed to the foreman, Seligmann, section K, road ix, workshop 743," said the sentinel. "You must follow the roundway to your right till you come to the K boundary, and there show yourself to the porter. Do you know the rule? Expelled, if you enter another section than your own," he added as the new-comer went away.

The young workman followed the direction indicated to him along the roadway. On his right lay a moat, above which marched numerous sentinels. On his left, between the wide circular road, and the mass of buildings, lay first a double line of railway, and then a second wall, similar to the outer one, which entirely surrounded the Steel City.

It was of so great an extent, that the sections, enclosed by the fortified walls like the spokes of a wheel, were perfectly independent of each other, although surrounded by the same wall and moat.

The young workman soon reached the boundary K,

placed at the side of the road, before a lofty gateway surmounted by the same letter sculptured in the stone, and presented himself to the porter.

This time, instead of having a soldier to deal with, he found himself before a pensioner, with a wooden leg, and medals on his breast.

The pensioner examined the paper, stamped it again and said—

"All right, ninth road on the left."

The young man entered this second intrenched line, and at last found himself in section K. The road which debouched from the gate was the axle, and at right angles on either side extended rows of uniform buildings.

The noise of machinery was almost deafening. Those grey buildings pierced with thousands of windows were like living monsters. But the new-comer was apparently accustomed to such scenes, for he bestowed not the slightest attention on the curious sight.

In five minutes he had found road ix, workshop 743, and having entered a little office full of portfolios and registers, stood in the presence of the foreman Seligmann.

The man took the paper with all its stamps, examined it, then looked the young workman up and down.

"Hired as puddler, are you?" he asked; "you seem very young?"

"Age has nothing to do with it," was the answer. "I

shall soon be six-and-twenty, and I've been puddling for the last seven months. If you like I can show you certificates on the strength of which I was engaged at New York by the head overseer."

The young man spoke German quite easily, but with a slight accent which seemed to arouse the suspicions of the foreman.

"Are you an Alsacian?" he demanded.

"No, I am Swiss—from Schaffhausen. "Look, here are all my papers, quite correct," he added, taking out a leather pocket-book and showing a passport, testimonial, and certificates.

"Very good. After all, you are hired, and it's my business simply to show you your place," returned Seligmann, assured by this display of official documents.

He then inscribed in a register the name of Johann Schwartz, copying it from the order, and gave to the workman a blue card bearing his name and the number 57,938, adding—

"You must be at the K gate every morning at seven o'clock; show this card which will already have passed you through the outer wall. Take from the rack in the lodge a counter with your number on it and show it to me when you come in. At seven in the evening, as you go out, drop the counter into a box placed at the door of the workshop, and only open at that time."

"I know the system. Can I live in the town?" asked Schwartz.

"No; you must find a lodging outside, but you can get your meals at the canteen in the shed at a very moderate price. Your wages are a dollar a day to begin with, but they will be raised quarterly. Expulsion is the only punishment. It is pronounced by me at first, and by the engineer on appeal, for any infraction of the rules. Will you begin to-day?"

"Why not?"

"It will be but half-a-day," observed the foreman, as he guided Schwartz to an inner gallery.

The two men walked along a wide passage, crossed a yard and entered a vast hall, like the platform of an immense terminus. Schwartz, as he glanced round, could not restrain a movement of professional admiration.

On each side of the long hall were two rows of enormous columns, as big as those in St. Peter's, at Rome, their tops rising through the glass roof. These were the chimneys of the puddling furnaces, and there were fifty of them in a row.

At one end engines were continually bringing up waggon loads of iron to feed the furnaces; at the other, empty trucks appeared to receive and carry away the metal, transformed into steel.

This metamorphosis is accomplished by means of the

operation of "puddling," at which gangs of half-naked Cyclops, armed with long iron rakes, were working with might and main.

The "pigs" of iron are thrown into a furnace brought to an intense heat. As soon as melted, the metal is stirred about for a considerable time. When it acquires a certain consistency, the puddler, by means of his long hook, turns and rolls about the molten mass, and makes it up into four blooms, or balls, which he then hands over to others.

The operation is continued in the midst of the hall. Opposite each furnace stands a shingling hammer, moved by steam.

Protected by boots and armlets of iron, the head covered with a metallic veil, and wearing a thick leathern apron, the "shingler" with his long pincers takes up the red hot ball, and places it under the hammer. Down on it comes the weight of the ponderous machine, pressing out a quantity of dross, amidst showers of sparks. When it cools it is taken back to the furnace, to be brought out again and hammered as before.

There was incessant movement in this monster forge. To a spectator it was a terrifying scene, the cascades of molten metal, dull blows heard above the roaring, showers of brilliant sparks, the glare of the red hot furnaces. In the fearful din and tumult, man appeared like a helpless infant.

Powerful fellows must these puddlers be. To stir and knead four hundredweight of metallic paste in that temperature, to see nothing for hours but the blinding glare of the furnace and molten iron, is trying work, and wears a man out in ten years.

Schwartz, as if to show the foreman what he could do, at once stripped off his coat and woollen shirt, exhibiting a well-knit frame, and arms on which the muscles stood out like cords, seized a hook which one of the puddlers had just put down, and set to work.

Seeing that he was likely to do well, the foreman soon left, and returned to his office.

The new-comer worked on until the dinner-hour. But he was either too energetic, or he had neglected to take sufficient food that morning to support his strength in this unusual toil, for he soon appeared tired and faint. Indeed so worn out did he seem that the chief of his gang noticed it.

"You're not fit for a puddler, my lad," he said, "and you had best ask at once to be changed into another section, for they won't do it later."

Schwartz protested against this. It was but a passing faintness. He could puddle as well as any one!

The gang's-man made his report however, and Schwartz was immediately called up before the chief engineer.

This personage examined his papers, shook his head, and asked in an inquisitorial tone—

"Were you a puddler at Brooklyn?"

The young man looked down in confusion.

"I must confess it, I see," he answered. "I was employed in casting, and it was in the hope of increasing my salary that I wished to try my hand at puddling."

"You are all alike," returned the engineer, shrugging his shoulders. "At five-and-twenty you think you can do what few men of five-and-thirty are fit for. Well, then, are you good at casting?"

"I was two months in the first class."

"You had better have stayed in it! Here you will have to begin in the third. All the same, you may think yourself lucky in being allowed to change your section so easily!"

The engineer then wrote a few words on a pass, sent a telegram, and said—

"Give up your counter, leave this division, and go straight to section O, chief engineer's office. He has been told."

The same formalities were gone through again that Schwartz had met with at the K gate. As in the morning, he was questioned, accepted, and sent to the foreman of the workshop, who introduced him into the casting-hall. But here the work was more silent, and more methodical.

"This is only a small gallery, for casting forty-two pounders," observed the foreman; "first-class workmen alone are allowed to cast the big guns."

The " small " gallery was not less than four hundred and fifty feet long and two hundred wide. Schwartz, as he glanced round, calculated that there must be at least six hundred crucibles being heated, by four, eight, or twelve together in the side furnaces.

The moulds destined for the reception of the fused steel were placed down the middle of the gallery, at the bottom of a trench. On each side of the trench was a movable crane, which, running on a line of rails, was constantly in use for moving enormous weights. As in the puddling hall, at one end was a railroad for the conveyance of the bars of steel, at the other, one for taking away the cannon as they came out of the mould.

Near each mould stood a man armed with an iron rod, to test the state of fusion of the metal in the crucibles.

The processes, which Schwartz had seen put in practice elsewhere, were here brought to a remarkable state of perfection.

When a cast was to be made, a warning bell gave the signal to all the watchers of the crucibles. Then, two by two, workmen of equal height, bearing between them on their shoulders a horizontal bar of iron, came with measured step, and placed themselves before every furnace.

An officer, armed with a whistle, his chronometer in his hand, stood near the mould, conveniently placed for all the furnaces in action. On each side, channels of refractory earth, covered with metal, converged in gentle slopes to a funnel-shaped reservoir, placed just above the mould. The officer whistled ; immediately a crucible, taken from the fire with pincers, was slung on the iron bar supported by the two workmen. The whistle commenced a series of modulations, and the two men, keeping time to it, approached and emptied the contents of their crucible into the corresponding channel. Then they tossed their empty, still red-hot receptacle into a vat.

Without interruption, at regular intervals, so as to keep up a constant flow, gangs from the other furnaces went through exactly the same operation.

It was all executed with such wonderful precision that just at the appointed time the last crucible was emptied and flung into the vat. The manœuvre seemed rather the result of a blind mechanism, than the co-operation of a hundred human wills.

Inflexible discipline, the force of habit, and the power of the measured musical strain, worked the miracle.

The sight appeared familiar to Schwartz, who was soon coupled with a man of his own height, tested in a small cast, and found a capital workman. Indeed, the head of his gang at the close of the day promised him a speedy rise.

On leaving the section O, at seven that evening, he went back to the inn to fetch his portmanteau. Then, following one of the exterior roads, he soon came to a group of houses, which he had remarked that morning as he passed, and easily found a lodging in the cottage of a good woman who "took in a lodger."

After supper, our young workman did not, like too many of his class, stroll out to the nearest public-house. He shut himself in his room, took from his pocket a fragment of steel evidently picked up in the puddling shed, a little crucible earth from the O section, and examined them carefully by the light of a smoky lamp. Then, taking from his portmanteau a thick manuscript book, half full of notes, receipts, and calculations, he wrote the following in good French, though, for precaution, in a cipher of which he alone knew the key:

" November 10th.—Stahlstadt.—There is nothing particular in the mode of puddling, unless, of course, it is the choice of two different temperatures, relatively low for the first heat and the re-heating, according to Chernoff's rules. As to the casting, it is done after Krupp's process, but with a perfectly admirable uniformity of movement. This precision in manœuvres is the great German power. It results from the innate musical talent in the German race. The English could never attain to this perfection; they have no ear, and want discipline. The French may reach it easily, as they are the most perfect dancers in the world. So far, there appears to be nothing mysterious in the

remarkable success of this manufacture.   The mineral
specimens which I picked up on the mountain are similar
to our best iron.

" The coal is certainly uncommonly fine, of an eminently
metallurgic quality, but still there is nothing unusual
in it.

" There is no doubt that in the Schwartz manufacture
special care is taken to purify the principal materials from
any foreign matter, that they may be employed only in a
perfectly pure state   The result may easily be imagined.
To be in possession of the remainder of the problem, I
have only to determine the composition of the refractory
earth of which the crucibles and the channels are made.
This discovered, and our gangs of workmen properly
drilled, I do not see why we should not do what they do
here.   All the same, as yet I have only seen two sections,
and there are at least four-and-twenty, without counting
the central building, the plans and models department,
the secret cabinet !   What dangerous schemes may not be
maturing in that den ?   What may not our friends have to
fear, after the threat uttered by Herr Schultz when he
took possession of his fortune ? "

After these questions, Schwartz, who was tired enough
with his day's work, undressed, laid himself down in a
little bed, which was about as uncomfortable as a German
bed could be—and that is saying a good deal—lighted

his pipe, and began to smoke, and read a well-worn book. But his thoughts were apparently elsewhere. The odorous clouds issued from his lips as if they were saying—

"Pooh! Pooh! Pooh! Pooh!"

He soon put down his book, and remained lost in thought for a long time, as if he were absorbed in the solution of a difficult problem.

"Ah," he exclaimed at last, "though the devil himself should try to prevent me I will find out the secret of Professor Schultz, and, above all, what he is meditating against Frankville!"

Schwartz went to sleep, murmuring the name of Doctor Sarrasin; but in his dreams it was the name of Jeannette, sweet little Jeannette, that was on his lips. He had never forgotten the little girl, although Jeannette, since he last saw her, had grown into a young lady. This phenomenon is easily explained by the ordinary laws of the association of ideas. Thoughts of the doctor brought up that of his daughter—association by contiguity. Then, when Schwartz—or rather Max Bruckmann—awoke, having still Jeannette in his mind, he was not at all astonished, but found in this fact a fresh proof of the excellence of the psychological principles of John Stuart Mill.

CHAPTER VI.

THE ALBRECHT PIT.

FRAU BAUER, Max Bruckmann's good landlady, was a
Swiss by birth, and widow of a miner, who was killed four
years previously in one of those accidents which make a
miner's life so precarious. She was allowed a small
annual pension of thirty dollars, and, in addition, the wages
of her boy Carl, brought regularly to her every Sunday.
She was enabled slightly to increase her income by letting
a furnished room.

Although scarcely thirteen, Carl was employed in the
coal mine as a trapper; it being his duty to open and
shut one of the ventilator doors, whenever it was necessary
for the coal trucks to pass. His mother had her house on
lease; and as it was too far from the Albrecht pit for him
to come home every evening, he had obtained some night
work at the bottom of the same mine. It was not heavy,
being merely to look after six horses, whilst the man

who had charge of them during the day spent the night above ground.

Carl's young life was passed, therefore, almost entirely, fifteen hundred feet below the surface of the earth. All day he kept watch by his door, all night he slept on a bed of straw, near his horses. On Sunday mornings only, did he return to the light of day, to revel for a few short hours in the universal blessing of the sun, the blue sky, and his mother's smile.

As may be imagined, after such a week, on coming up from the pit he was hardly what would be called presentable. Indeed he was more like a young gnome, a sweep, or a negro, than anything else. Frau Bauer had always a large supply of hot water and soap ready, and devoted a good hour, the first thing, to scrubbing him. She next dressed him in a comfortable suit of dark green cloth, made from an old one of his father's, and kept all the week in the big deal cupboard, and then set to work to admire her boy, an occupation of which she never tired, for she thought him the handsomest in the world.

When the layer of coal-dust was washed off, Carl was really as good-looking as most boys. His golden silky locks, his pleasant blue eyes, well suited his fair complexion, but he was altogether too small for his age. His sunless life made him as white as a turnip and, had Dr. Sarrasin's compte-globules been applied to the blood of the young

miner, it would probably have revealed that he possessed a
very insufficient quantity.

In character he was rather silent and quiet, with some of
that pride which the feeling of constant danger, the habit of
regular work, and the satisfaction of difficulties overcome,
gives to all miners.

His greatest happiness was to sit near his mother at the
square table in their little kitchen, and arrange in a box a
large number of frightful insects brought from the bowels
of the earth. The warm and equal atmosphere of the
mines has its special fauna, little known by naturalists, just
as the damp walls of the pits have their flora of curious
mosses, mushrooms, and lichens.

The engineer, Maulesmülhe, who was fond of entomology,
had remarked this, and had promised a small reward for
each new specimen that Carl brought him. This, which
had at first led the boy to explore all the recesses of the
mine, had gradually taught him to be a collector. He now
sought for insects on his own account.

However, he did not limit his affections to spiders and
wood-lice. He was on intimate terms with two bats and a
big rat. If he was to be believed, these three animals were
the most intelligent and amiable creatures in the world ;
even more intellectual than the horses with long silky
manes and shining sides, of which Carl always spoke in
terms of warm admiration.

Blair-Athol was chief favourite, the eldest in the stable, a philosophical old horse, who had been for six years fifteen hundred feet below the level of the sea, and had all that time never seen the light of day. He was now nearly blind.

But how well he knew his way along the subterranean labyrinth, when to turn to the right or when to the left, as he drew his trucks, without ever missing a step! He always stopped at the right time before the trap, leaving just room enough to open it. In what a friendly way did he neigh, morning and evening, at the exact minute when it was time for his provender to be brought him. How good, how obedient, how gentle, he was!

" I declare, mother, he really gives me a kiss, by rubbing his cheek against mine, when I put my head near him," said Carl. "And he is wonderfully useful besides, mind you, for he is just like a clock ; without him we should never know whether it was night or day, morning or evening."

So chattered the boy, and dame Bauer listened to him with delight. She, too, loved Blair-Athol as much as her son did, and never failed to send him a lump of sugar. She would have given anything to go and see the old servant her husband had known, and at the same time visit the dismal place where poor Bauer's body—black as ink, carbonised by the fire-damp—had been found after the explosion. But women are not admitted into the mines, and she had to be satisfied with the vivid descriptions given by her son.

Ah! she knew that mine well—that great dark pit to
which her husband went down, and never returned. How
many times she had waited near the yawning mouth,
eighteen feet in diameter, looking along the walling of freestone, gazing at the oaken frame-work to which the corves
were drawn up by cables and pulleys of steel—visited the
out-works, the engine-shed, the scorer's hut, and the rest!
How many times had she warmed herself at the glowing
brazier where the miners dry their garments on emerging
from the pit, and the impatient smokers light their pipes!
How familiar she was with all the noise and activity of the
place!

The receivers who unhooked the loaded corves—the
sorters, washers, engine-men, stokers—she had watched
them all at work over and over again.

What she could not see, and yet could always picture
with the eyes of affection, was what happened when the
basket sank down, carrying its cluster of workmen, with
formerly her husband, and now her only child among them.

She could hear their voices and laughter, growing fainter
and fainter in the depths, and finally ceasing altogether.
In her thoughts she followed that frail basket as it was
lowered—down, down the narrow chimney, fifteen, eighteen
hundred feet,—fourteen times the height of the great
pyramid, till it arrived at the bottom, and the men hastened
off to their work.

She imagined them all dispersing to different parts of the subterranean town, some to the right, some to the left—pickers, armed with strong pickaxes to attack the blocks of coal; shorers, to bank up places whence the coal had been hollowed; carpenters, to put up wood-work; labourers, to repair the roads and lay down rails; masons, to cement the roofs.

A wide central gallery led from this shaft to another, a ventilator about a mile distant. At right angles from this spread secondary roads; and in parallel lines, smaller ones again. These roads were separated by walls and pillars of coal or rock. All was regular, square, solid, black!

And this labyrinth of roads was alive with half-naked miners, working, talking, laughing, by the light of their safety-lamps.

All this dame Bauer could see, as she sat alone, dreaming, beside her fire.

Among the numerous galleries, the one she oftenest imagined to herself was where her boy Carl opened and shut his door.

When evening came, the day workmen went up, to be replaced by others; but her boy did not go with the rest to take his place in the basket. He went off to the stable, patted his beloved Blair-Athol, and gave him his supper of oats and fresh hay. Then he ate his own little cold supper, which had been sent to him, played for a few minutes with his big pet rat, caught and stroked the two bats as they fluttered about him, and then was soon fast asleep on his heap of straw.

Well did the fond mother know all this, and much she loved to hear every incident of her boy's daily life.

"Mother, what do you think Mr. Maulesmülhe, the engineer, said to me yesterday? He said that if I gave correct answers to some questions in arithmetic which he would put to me one of these days, he would take me to hold the land-chain when he surveys the mine with his compass. It seems they are going to pierce a new gallery, to join the Weber shaft, and he will find it uncommonly difficult to bring it out in the right place!"

"Really!" cried dame Bauer with delight; "did Mr. Maulesmülhe say that!" And already she imagined her Carl holding the chain along the gallery, whilst the engineer, note-book in hand, set down figures, and, his eyes fixed on the compass, ordered the direction of the opening.

"Unluckily," continued Carl, "I have nobody to explain what I don't understand in my arithmetic, and I'm much afraid I shall not answer correctly!"

At this point, Max, who was silently smoking by the fireside, which place, as a lodger in the house, he had the privilege of occupying, joined in the conversation, and said to the boy—

" If you like to show me what you find difficult, perhaps I can give you a helping hand."

" You ? " said dame Bauer with some incredulity.

" Certainly," replied Max. " Do you think I learn nothing at the evening class to which I go regularly after supper ? The master is very pleased with me, and says he will make me a monitor."

This settled, Max brought from his room a clean paper copy-book, and seating himself by the lad, explained the difficult sum, with so much clearness that the astonished Carl managed it easily.

From that day dame Bauer showed more consideration for her lodger, and Max took a great liking to his little companion.

In the factory, Max showed himself an exemplary workman, and was not long in being promoted to the second, and then to the first class. Every morning he was at the O gate punctually at seven o'clock. Every evening, after his supper, he repaired to the class taught by the engineer, Trubner. Geometry, algebra, drawing of diagrams and machines—he attacked them all with equal ardour; and his progress was so rapid that his master was much struck by it. Two months from his entry into the Schultz manufactory, the young workman was already noted as one of the cleverest intellects, not only in the A section, but in all Stahlstadt. A report of his engineer, sent up at the end of the quarter, bore this formal mention :

" Schwartz (Johann) twenty-six, working caster of the first class. I wish to bring this man before the notice of the Directors, as quite above the average, in three respects, theoretical knowledge, practical skill, and remarkable genius for invention."

But something more than this was required to draw the attention of the chiefs to Max. It was not long in coming; though unfortunately it was under the most tragical circumstances.

One Sunday morning, Max, much astonished at hearing ten o'clock strike without his young friend Carl having appeared, went down to ask dame Bauer if she knew any reason for this delay. He found her very uneasy; Carl ought to have been at home two hours and more. Seeing her anxiety, Max offered to go and look after him, and set off in the direction of the Albrecht shaft.

He met several miners on the way, and inquired from them if they had seen the boy ; then, on receiving a negative reply, exchanging the " Glück auf!" (success to you! safe return!), which is the usual salutation of German pitmen, Max continued his walk.

About eleven o'clock, he reached the head of the Albrecht shaft. It was not noisy, and animated, as on a week day; there was only one young "milliner," as the mineis jokingly call the sorters of the coal—chatting with the watchman, whose duty kept him, even on this day, at the pit's mouth.

" Have you seen little Carl Bauer, number 41,902, come up this morning ? " asked Max of this functionary.

The man consulted his list, and shook his head.

" Is there any other outlet to the mine ? "

" No, this is the only one ; the new shaft to the north is not yet finished."

" Then, is the boy below ? "

" He must be, though it's an odd thing too, for on Sundays only the five watchmen should be left.'

" Can I go down to find out ? "

" Not without permission."

" There may have been an accident," put in the milliner.

" Not possible on Sunday."

" All the same," said Max, " I must find out what has become of that boy."

" You must speak to the overseer of machinery, in his office, if he is still there."

The overseer, dressed in his Sunday best, with a shirt collar as stiff as if it had been made out of tin, was fortunately still at his accounts. He was an intelligent and humane man, and at once entered into Max's anxiety.

" We will go immediately and see what he is doing."

And ordering the man on duty to be ready to pay away
the cable, he prepared to descend into the mine with the
young workman.

"Have you not the Galibert apparatus?" asked Max.
"It may be useful."

"You are right. One can never be sure what has
occurred at the bottom of the pit."

Saying this, the overseer took from a cupboard two zinc
reservoirs, similar to the urns which the street cocoa-sellers
in Paris carry on their backs. These were boxes of com-
pressed air, placed in communication with the lips by
means of two india-rubber tubes, the horn mouthpiece
being held between the teeth. They are filled with the aid
of peculiar bellows, constructed to empty themselves completely. The nose being held in wooden pincers, a man
may, thus supplied with a store of air, penetrate into the
most unbreathable atmosphere.

These preparations completed, the overseer and Max
took their places in the basket, the cable moved, and the
descent began.

Two small electric lamps shed some degree of light
around, and the men conversed together as they were
lowered into the depths of the earth.

"For a man not in the business you are a cool hand,"
remarked the overseer. "I've seen people who couldn't
summon up courage enough to go down; or if they

did, they crouched like rabbits at the bottom of the basket all the time."

"Really," answered Max, "it seems nothing to me; though it's true I have been down a coal mine two or three times before."

They were soon landed at the foot of the shaft. The watchman whom they found there had seen nothing of young Carl.

They first visited the stable; the horses were there alone, and appeared quite tired of their own company. At least such was the conclusion to be drawn from the neigh with which Blair-Athol greeted the approach of the three human figures. On a nail hung Carl's knapsack, and in a corner, beside a curry-comb, lay his arithmetic book.

Max remarked directly that his lantern was not there, a fresh proof that the boy must be still in the mine.

" He may have been hurt by a landslip," said the over· seer, "but it is scarcely probable. What can he have been doing in the galleries on a Sunday ?"

" Oh ! perhaps he went to hunt for some insects before going up," said the watchman. " It is quite a passion with him."

The stable-boy, who arrived in the midst of this discussion, confirmed this supposition. He had seen Carl start at seven o'clock with his lantern.

A regular search was immediately commenced. The

other watchmen were called, and each one, with his lantern,
told off in a different direction, pointed out to him on a
large plan of the mine, that every tunnel and gallery
might be thoroughly examined.

In two hours the whole mine had been gone through, and
the seven men met again at the foot of the shaft. There
had not been the least appearance of a landslip found any-
where, nor the least trace of Carl. The overseer, perhaps
influenced by an increasing appetite, inclined to the opinion
that the boy had passed out unperceived, and would by
this time be at his home. But Max, convinced of the
contrary, insisted on renewed exertions.

"What is that ?" he asked, pointing to a dotted region on
the plan, resembling in the midst of the adjacent minute-
ness those terræ incognitæ marked on the confines of the
arctic continents.

"That is the zone provisionally deserted, because of the
thinning of the bed," replied the overseer.

"Is there a deserted zone? We must look there!"
exclaimed Max, with a decision to which the other men
submitted.

They were not long in reaching the entrance to some
galleries which, to judge by the slimy and mouldy walls,
might have been deserted for many years.

They had proceeded for some time without coming upon
anything suspicious, when Max stopped, and said—

POOR LITTLE CARL.   [*Page* 93.

" Do you not feel stupefied, and attacked with headache ?"

" Why, yes, indeed we do !" answered his companions.

" So do I," resumed Max; " for a moment I felt quite giddy. There is certainly carbonic acid gas about ! Will you allow me to light a match ?" he asked of the overseer.

" By all means, my lad, strike away."

Max took his little box from his pocket, struck a match, and stooping, held it towards the ground, upon which it instantly went out.

" I was sure of it," he remarked. " The gas, being more heavy than the air, lies close to the ground. You must not stay here—I mean those who have not the Galibert apparatus. If you like, sir, we can continue the search alone."

This being agreed to, Max and the overseer each took between his teeth the mouthpiece of his air box, placed the nippers on his nostrils, and boldly penetrated into a succession of old galleries.

In a quarter of an hour they came out to renew the air in their reservoirs ; this done, they started again.

On the third trial their efforts were crowned with success. The faint bluish light of an electric lamp was seen far off in the darkness. They hastened to it.

At the foot of the damp wall, motionless and already cold, lay poor little Carl. His blue lips and sunken eyes told what had happened.

He had evidently wished to pick up something from the ground, had stooped, and been literally drowned in the carbonic acid gas.

Every effort to recall him to life was in vain. He must have been already dead four or five hours. By the next evening there was another little grave in the cemetery of Stahlstadt, and poor dame Bauer was bereaved of her child as well as of her husband.

CHAPTER VII.

THE CENTRAL BLOCK.

A REPORT from Dr. Echternach, surgeon-in-chief to the section of the Albrecht pit, stated that the death of Carl Bauer, number 41,902, thirteen years of age, trapper in gallery 228, was caused by asphyxia, resulting from the absorption by the respiratory organs of a large proportion of carbonic acid.

Another no less luminous report from the engineer Maulesmülhe, explained the necessity of including in the ventilating scheme zone B in the plan xiv., as a large amount of deleterious gas filtered slowly from its galleries. Lastly, a note from the same functionary brought before the notice of the authorities the devotedness of the overseer Rayer, and of the first-class workman, Johann Schwartz.

Ten hours later, on reaching the porter's lodge, Max, as he took his presence-counter, found this printed order on the nail, addressed to him :

" Schwartz will present himself at the Director-General's office at ten o'clock to-day. Central block, Gate and Road A."

"At last!" thought Max. "This is the first step; the rest will come!"

While chatting with his comrades on his Sunday walks round Stahlstadt, he had acquired sufficient knowledge of the general organisation of the city to know that authority to enter the central block was not to be had every day. All sorts of stories were current about this place. It was said that some indiscreet people, who had tried to get into the guarded enclosure by stratagem, had never been seen again. That before their admission, all workmen employed there had to go through a series of masonic ceremonies—were obliged to take the most solemn oaths not to reveal anything that went on there, and were mercilessly sentenced to death by a secret tribunal if they violated their oath. A subterranean railway put this sanctuary in communication with the out-works. Night trains brought unknown visitors. Supreme councils were held there, and sometimes mysterious personages came to participate in the deliberations.

Without putting unnecessary faith in these accounts, Max knew that they were really the popular expression of a well-known fact—the extreme difficulty which attended admission into the central division. Of all the workmen whom he knew—and he had friends in the iron mines as well as in the coal pits, among the refiners as well as the men employed in the blast furnaces, among the carpenters as well as the smiths—not one had ever entered the gate.

It was therefore with a feeling of intense curiosity as well as secret pleasure that he presented himself there at the hour named. It was soon plain that the precautions were of the strictest.

Evidently Max was expected. Two men, dressed in a grey uniform, swords at their sides, and revolvers in their belts, were waiting in the porter's lodge.

This lodge, like that of a cloistered convent, had two gates, an outer and an inner one, which were never open at the same time.

The pass examined and signed, Max saw, though without manifesting any surprise, a white handkerchief brought out, with which the two attendants in uniform carefully bandaged his eyes.

Then taking him by the arms, they marched him off without saying a word.

After walking two or three thousand steps they mounted a staircase, a door was opened and shut, and Max was allowed to take off his bandage.

He found himself in a large plain room, furnished with some chairs, a black board, and a long desk, supplied with

every implement necessary for linear drawing. It was
lighted by high windows, filled with ground glass.

Almost immediately, two personages, who looked as if
they belonged to a university, entered the room.

" You are brought before our notice as having somewhat
distinguished yourself," said one of them. " We are about
to examine you to find out if there is reason to admit you
into the model division. Are you prepared to answer our
questions ?"

Max modestly declared himself ready to be put to the
proof.

The two examiners then successively put questions to
him in chemistry, geometry, and algebra. The young
workman satisfied them in every case by the clearness and
precision of his answers. The figures which he traced in
chalk on the board were neat, decided, and elegant. His
equations in the most perfect way, in equal lines, like the
ranks of a crack regiment. One of these demonstrations
was so remarkable, and so new to the judges, that they
expressed their astonishment, and asked where he had
been taught.

" At Schaffhaüsen, my native town, in the elementary
school."

" You appear a good draughtsman ?"

" It was my strong point."

" The education given in Switzerland is decidedly very

uncommon," remarked one examiner to the other. "We will give you two hours to execute this," he resumed, handing to the candidate a drawing of a very complicated-looking steam-engine. "If you acquit yourself well you shall be admitted with the mention, 'Perfectly satisfactory and very superior.'"

Left alone, Max set eagerly to work.

When his judges re-entered at the expiration of the given time, they were so delighted with his diagram, that they added to the promised mention, "We have not another draughtsman of equal talent."

Our young workman was then again seized by the grey attendants, and with the same ceremonial, that is to say, the bandaged eyes, was led to the office of the Director-General.

"You are offered admission to one of the studios in the model division," said this personage. "Are you ready to submit to the rules and regulations?"

"I do not know what they are," said Max; "but I presume they are acceptable."

"They are these: First, you are compelled, as long as your engagement lasts, to reside in the same division. You cannot go out but by special and exceptional order. Second, you are subjected to military discipline; and you owe absolute obedience, under military penalties, to your superiors. To weigh against this, you are also like the noncommissioned officers of an active army, for you may, by a regular advance, be raised to the highest grades. Third, you bind yourself by an oath never to reveal to any one what you see in the division to which you have access. Fourth, your correspondence is opened by your chiefs, all you send as well as all you receive; and it must be limited to your family."

"In short, I am in prison," thought Max.

Then he replied quietly—

"These rules seem perfectly just, and I am ready to submit to them."

"Good. Raise your hand. Take the oath. You are nominated draughtsman to the fourth studio. A lodging will be assigned to you, and for your meals, you will find a first-rate canteen here. You have not your property with you?"

"No, sir. As I was ignorant of what I was wanted for, I left everything in my room."

"They will be brought to you, for you must not again go out of the division."

"I did well," thought Max, "to write my notes in cipher! They would only have had to look at them!"

Before the close of the day, Max was established in a pretty little room, in the fourth story of a building over-looking a wide courtyard, and had some ideas about his new life.

He did not fancy that it would be as dismal as at first sight it appeared. His comrades, with whom he made acquaintance at the restaurant, were in general quiet and gentle, like all industrious people. To enliven themselves a little—for there was rather a want of gaiety in their mechanical life—they formed a band amongst themselves, and performed selections of very tolerable music every evening. A library, a reading-room, were valuable resources for the mind, from a scientific point of view, during the rare hours of leisure. Special courses held by professors were obligatory to all the men employed, who had besides to undergo frequent examinations and competitions. But fresh air and liberty were lacking in these narrow confines.

It was a regular college, only with extra strictness exercised on grown men. The surrounding atmosphere could not but weigh on their spirits, subjected as they were to an iron discipline.

The winter passed away in these employments, to which Max gave himself up heart and soul. His application, the perfection of his drawings, his extraordinary progress in every subject he was taught, noticed by all his tutors and examiners, had made for him, even in this short time, and amongst all these diligent men, a corresponding celebrity. By general consent he was the most clever draughtsman, the most ingenious, the most fruitful in resources. Was there a difficulty? they applied to him. Even the chiefs themselves resorted to his experience, with the respect which merit extorts even from the most marked jealousy.

But if, on reaching the heart of the model division, the young man calculated that he would be any nearer getting at the innermost secrets, he was very much out in his reckoning.

His life at present was enclosed within an iron railing three hundred yards in diameter, surrounding the segment of the central block to which he was attached. Intellectually, his activity could and should extend to the highest branches of metallurgic industry. In practice, it was limited to drawing steam-engines. He constructed them of all dimensions and of all powers, for every kind of industry and use, for war-ships and for printing-presses; but he never left this speciality. The division of labour pushed to its utmost limit held him as in a vice.

After four months passed in section A, Max knew no more of the entire plan of the works in the Steel City than he did on entering. At the most he had merely collected a little general information about the organisation of the machinery of which he formed—notwithstanding his merits—but a very small portion. He knew that the centre of the spider's web, figurative of Stahlstadt, was the Bull Tower, a kind of cyclopean structure, overlooking all the neighbouring buildings.

He had learnt, too, through the legendary stories of the canteen, that the dwelling of Herr Schultz himself was at the base of this tower, and that the renowned secret room occupied the centre. It was added that this vaulted hall, protected against any danger of fire, and plated inside, as a monitor is plated outside, was closed by a system of steel doors with spring-gun locks, worthy of the most suspicious bank. The general opinion was that Professor Schultz was working at the completion of a terrible engine of war of unprecedented power, and destined to assure universal dominion to Germany.

Max had revolved in his brain many most audacious plans of escalade and disguise, but had been compelled to acknowledge to himself that nothing of the sort was practicable. Those lines of sombre and massive walls, flooded with light during the night, and guarded by trusty sentinels, would always oppose an insuperable obstacle to every attempt. But even if he did overcome it to some extent what would he see? Details, always details, never the whole!

What matter! He had sworn not to yield, and he would not yield. If it took ten years, he would wait that time. But the hour was coming when that secret would be his own. It must! The happy city Frankville was prospering, its beneficent institutions favouring each and all, and giving a new horizon of hope to a disheartened people. Max had no doubt that in the face of such a triumph to the Latin race, Schultz would be more than ever determined to make good his threats. Stahlstadt and its factories were a proof of that.

Thus many weeks passed away.

One day in March, Max had just for the hundredth time repeated his secret vow, when one of the grey attendants informed him that the Director-General wished to speak to him.

"I have received from Herr Schultz," said this high functionary, "an order to send him our best draughtsman. You are the man. Make your arrangements to pass into the inner circle. You are promoted to the rank of lieutenant."

Thus, at the very moment when he was almost despairing of success, his heroic toil at last procured him the much desired entrance !

Max was so filled with delight that his joy exhibited itself on his countenance.

"I am happy to have such good news to announce to you," continued the Director ; "and I cannot refrain from urging you to continue in the path you have begun to tread so gallantly. A brilliant future is before you. Go, sir."

So Max, after his long probation, caught the first glimpse of the end which he had sworn to reach !

To stuff all his clothes into his portmanteau, follow the grey men, pass through the last enclosure, of which the entrance in the A road might have been still forbidden to him, was the work of a few minutes.

He now stood at the foot of the inaccessible Bull Tower ; until this moment he had but seen its lofty head reared among the clouds.

The scene which lay before him was indeed an unexpected one. Imagine a man suddenly transported from a noisy, commonplace European workshop into the midst of a virgin forest in the torrid zone. Such was the surprise which awaited Max in the centre of Stahlstadt.

As a virgin forest gains in beauty from the descriptions of great writers, so was Professor Schultz's park more beautiful than the most lovely of pleasure gardens. Slender palms, tufted bananas, curious cacti formed the shrubberies, Creepers wound gracefully round eucalyptus trees, hung in green festoons, or fell in rich clusters. The most tender plants bloomed in abundance. Pineapples and guavas ripened beside oranges. Humming-birds and birds of paradise displayed their brilliant plumage in the open air ; for the temperature was as tropical as the vegetation.

Max instinctively looked around and above for glass and hot-air pipes to account for this miracle ; seeing nothing but the blue sky he stopped bewildered.

Then it flashed upon him that not far from the spot was

a coal mine in permanent combustion, and he guessed that Herr Schultz had ingeniously utilised this valuable subterranean heat, by means of metallic pipes, to maintain a constant hot-house atmosphere.

But this explanation did not prevent the young Alsacian's eyes from being dazzled and charmed with the green lawns, while his nostrils inhaled with delight the delicious scents which filled the air. To a man who had passed six months without seeing even a blade of grass, it was truly refreshing. A gravelled path led him, by a gentle slope, to the foot of a handsome flight of marble steps, commanded by a majestic colonnade. Behind rose the huge and massive square building, which was as it were the pedestal of the Bull Tower.

Beneath the peristyle Max could see seven or eight servants in red livery, and a gorgeous porter in cocked hat, and bearing a halberd. And he noticed between the columns rich bronze candelabra. As he ascended the steps a slight rumble betrayed that the underground railroad lay beneath his feet.

Max gave his name, and was immediately admitted into a hall, a regular museum of sculpture. Not having time to examine anything, he was conducted first through a saloon, adorned with black and gold, then through one with red and gold ornaments, and he was finally left alone for five minutes in a yellow and gold saloon. At the end of that time a footman returned and showed him into a splendid green and gold study.

Herr Schultz in person, smoking a long clay pipe, with a tankard of beer at his side, had the effect, in the midst of all this luxury, of a spot of mud on a patent-leather boot.

Without rising, without even turning his head, the King of Steel merely said, in a cold tone—

"Are you the draughtsman?"

"Yes, sir."

"I have seen your diagrams. They are very good. But do you only understand steam-engines?"

"I have never been examined in anything else."

"Do you know anything of the science of projectiles?"

"I have studied it in my spare time, and for my own pleasure."

This reply interested Herr Schultz.

He deigned to turn and look at his employé.

"Well, will you undertake to design a cannon with me? We shall see what you can make of it! Ah! you will be scarcely able to take the place of that idiot of a Sohne, who got killed this morning whilst handling some dynamite! The fool might have blown us all up!"

It must be acknowledged that this revolting want of feeling was only what might have been expected from the mouth of Herr Schultz.

CHAPTER VIII.

THE DRAGON'S DEN.

THE reader who has followed the progress of our young Alsacian's fortune will probably not be much surprised to find him, at the end of a few weeks, firmly established in Herr Schultz's favour. The two had become inseparable. They worked together, they ate and walked together, and together they sat smoking over their foaming glasses of beer. The ex-professor of Jena had never before met with a coadjutor so entirely after his own heart, one who caught his meaning with half a word, and who could so rapidly utilise his theoretical ideas.

Max not merely possessed transcendent merit in all branches of the profession, he was besides the most charming companion, the most diligent worker, the most modestly fertile inventor.

Herr Schultz was delighted with him. Ten times a day

he said to himself, "What a treasure! what a pearl this fellow is!"

The truth was that Max had, at the first glance, seen through the character of his formidable patron, and perceiving that blind and insatiable vanity was its leading feature, he regulated his conduct by humouring the egotism which he despised.

In a few days the young man had acquired such skill in the fingering necessary for this human keyboard, that he could play upon Schultz as easily as one plays on a piano.

His tactics merely consisted in exhibiting his own merits to advantage, but always in such a way as to leave an opening for his master to show superiority over him. For instance, when he finished a drawing he would 'leave it perfect, with the exception of some slight fault, as easy to see as to correct, and this the ex-professor immediately and exultantly pounced upon.

Had he some theoretical idea, he caused it so to open out in the course of conversation that Herr Schultz might fancy that he himself had originated it. Sometimes he even went further, boldly saying—

"I have traced that plan of a vessel with the detached ram, which you asked for."

"I?" returned Herr Schultz, who had never dreamt of such a thing.

"Why, yes! you don't mean to say you have forgotten? A detached ram, which will leave a spindle-shaped torpedo in the enemy's side, to burst after an interval of three minutes!"

"I had not the least recollection of it. That comes of having a head like mine! it is so full of inventive genius that I forget my own ideas." And Herr Schultz conscientiously pocketed the credit of the new invention.

Perhaps, after all, he was only half duped by this artifice. In his innermost heart he probably felt that Max was stronger than he. But by one of those mysterious workings which go on in the human brain, he was contented with the appearance of superiority as long as he could delude his subordinate.

"But the fellow must be an ass after all, in spite of his cleverness!" he would sometimes say to himself, with a silent laugh which showed all the thirty-two dominoes in his jaw.

His vanity, if ever wounded, was soon consoled by the reflection that he alone in all the world could carry out these inventions and ideas. They would have been of no value but for his gold. After all Max was only part of the mechanism which he, Schultz, had set going, &c., &c.

Yet, although in high favour, Max was never taken into the professor's confidence, and after five months' sojourn in the Bull Tower, he knew little more than at first of its mysteries. His suspicions had become certainties, and that was all. He was now convinced that Stahlstadt contained a secret, and that Herr Schultz had some aim far beyond that of gain. The nature of his occupations rendered the supposition that he had invented some perfectly new engine of warfare extremely probable.

But the enigma had still to be solved. Max at last came to the conclusion that it would be impossible to obtain the knowledge he sought without coming to some crisis, and this he resolved to provoke.

It was after dinner on the evening of the 5th of September; exactly a year since he had found the body of his little friend Carl in the Albrecht pit.

Outside, the long severe American winter already covered the country with its white mantle; but in the park of Stahlstadt the temperature was as warm as during June, and the snow, melting before it touched the ground, fell in rain instead of flakes.

" Those sausages in sourkraut were delicious, were they not?" remarked Herr Schultz, whose love of his favourite dish was unaffected by the Begum's millions.

"Delicious!" returned Max, who had heroically partaken of this mess every evening, till at last he hated the very sight of it.

His feelings on this subject decided him at once to carry his meditated project into execution.

"I wonder," resumed Herr Schultz, with a sigh, "how people who have neither sausages, nor sourkraut, nor beer, can endure existence."

"Life must be one long misery to them," replied Max. "It would really be a charity to unite all mankind with the Vaterland."

"Well! well! that will come, that will come!" exclaimed the King of Steel. "Here we are already installed in the heart of America. Just let us take an island or two in the neighbourhood of Japan, and you will see in what a few strides we shall get round the globe!"

The footman now brought in the pipes; Herr Schultz filled and lighted his. Max had purposely determined to make use of this moment of supreme bliss, so began, after a few minutes' silence—

"I must say that I don't quite believe in this conquest!"

"What conquest?" asked Herr Schultz, who had forgotten what was the topic of conversation.

"The conquest of the world by the Germans."

The ex-professor thought he had not heard correctly.

"You do not believe in the conquest of the world by the Germans?"

"No."

"Oh, indeed, that is something strange! I am curious to know the reasons for your doubt."

'Simply because the French artillerymen will end by

doing better, and will far surpass you. The Swiss, my fellow-countrymen, who know them well, are firmly convinced that a forewarned Frenchman is worth two Germans. The lesson of 1870 will be repeated against those who gave it. No one doubts this in my little country, sir, and if I may venture to say so, it is the opinion of the cleverest men in England."

Max had uttered these words in a cool, dry, and decisive tone, which, if it were possible, doubled the effect of the point-blank blasphemy.

Herr Schultz glared wildly—his astonishment almost choked him. Then the blood rushed to his face with such violence that the young man feared, for a moment, he had gone too far. However, seeing that rage had not stifled his victim, and that he would not die of the shock this time, he resumed—

"Yes, it is annoying to think of; but it's the fact. Although our rivals make no noise about it, yet they are working. Do you think they have learnt nothing since the war? Whilst we are stupidly trying to increase the weight of our cannon, you may be certain that they are preparing something new, and that we shall see what it is on the very first opportunity!"

"Something new, something new!" stammered Herr Schultz. "We are doing that too, sir!"

"Ah, yes, in a way. We are making in steel what our

predecessors made in bronze, that's all. We double the proportions and the range of our pieces."

"Double!" exclaimed Herr Schultz, in a tone which signified, "Indeed! we do better than double!"

"In short," resumed Max, "we are mere plagiarists. See here, the truth is we lack any genius for inventing. We discover nothing, and the French do, and will, you may be sure."

Herr Schultz had become, outwardly at least, rather calmer, though his trembling lips, and the paleness which had succeeded the apoplectic crimson, betrayed the agitated state of his mind.

Must he endure such a pitch of humiliation? To be the far-famed Schultz, the absolute master of the greatest manufactory and cannon foundry in the whole world, to have kings and parliaments at his feet, and then to be told by an insignificant Swiss draughtsman that he lacked invention, that he was below a French gunner! And all this when he had close to him, on the other side of a plated wall, something which would a thousand times confound the impudent rascal, shut him up completely, and sweep away all his idiotic arguments? No, it was not to be endured!

Herr Schultz rose so abruptly that he broke his pipe. Then, casting at Max a glance full of irony, he hissed out from between his set teeth—

"Follow me, sir, I am about to show you whether I, Herr Schultz, have any lack of invention!"

Max had played high, but had won—thanks to the surprise his bold and unexpected language had produced, and the passion he had aroused.

Vanity being stronger than prudence with the ex-professor, Schultz was now eager to lay open his secret. He led the way with a hurried step into his study, closed the door carefully, and walking straight up to the bookcase, touched a panel. Immediately an opening, concealed by the rows of books, appeared in the wall. This was the entrance to a narrow passage, leading by a stone staircase to the very foot of the Bull Tower.

There, an oaken door was opened by means of a little key, which never left the possession of the master of the place. A second door appeared, fastened with a padlock, similar to those used for strong boxes.

Herr Schultz threw open the heavy iron barrier, protected within by a complicated apparatus of explosive machinery, which Max, actuated by professional curiosity, would have much liked to examine; but his guide left him no time to do so.

The two men then found themselves before a third door, without any apparent lock or bolt, which yielded to a slight push, given, however, in a particular way.

This third barrier passed, Herr Schultz and his companion

climbed an iron staircase of two hundred steps, and arrived
at the summit of the Bull Tower, overlooking all the city of
Stahlstadt.

In the centre of a sort of casemate, pierced with numerous
embrasures, stood a steel cannon.

"There!" exclaimed the professor, who had not uttered
a word since they left the dining-room.

It was the most enormous piece of ordnance Max had
ever beheld. A breach-loader of at least three hundred tons.
Its mouth measured nearly five feet in diameter. Mounted
on a steel carriage, and running on rails of the same metal,
it might have been manœuvred by a child, so easy were all
its movements made, by a system of cogged wheels. A
spring, fixed at the back of the carriage, had the effect of
annulling the recoil, or at least producing a perfectly equal
reaction, so that after each shot the gun returned to its
first position.

"And what may be the perforating power of this piece?"
asked Max, who could not restrain his admiration.

"At twenty thousand yards we can pierce a forty-inch
plate as easily as if it were a slice of bread and butter!"

"And its range?"

"Its range?" cried Schultz, enthusiastically. "Ah!
you said just now that our imitative genius had done
nothing more than double the range of former guns!
Well, with this fellow, I would undertake to send, with

THE MASTERPIECE OF HERR SCHULTZ. [*Page* 116.

tolerable precision, a projectile to the distance of thirty miles!"

"Thirty miles!" cried Max. "Thirty miles! What new powder can you use?"

"Oh! I can tell you everything, now," replied Herr Schultz, in a peculiar tone. "There is no inconvenience in revealing my secrets to you. Large grained powder has served its time. Gun-cotton is what I use; its expansive power is four times that of ordinary powder, and I increase it fivefold by mixing with it eight-tenths of its weight of nitrate of potash."

"But," observed Max, "no piece, though made of the best steel, could stand that long. After four or five shots your cannon will be impaired, and soon become useless."

"If it were only to fire one shot that one would be sufficient!"

"It would be an expensive one."

"It would cost a million, for that is the net cost of the gun."

"One shot worth a million!"

"What matter, so that it destroyed a thousand millions!"

"A thousand millions!" cried Max.

"However, he restrained the mingled horror and admiration with which this fearful agent of destruction inspired him, and added—

"It is assuredly a wonderful and astonishing piece of

artillery, but, notwithstanding its merits, it bears out my
theory, there are improvements certainly, but it is all
imitation, no invention."

"No invention!" responded Herr Schultz, shrugging his
shoulders. "I repeat that I have now no secrets from you.
Come with me."

"The King of Steel and his companion then left the
casemate and descended to a lower story, by means of an
hydraulic lift. Here lay a large number of long objects,
cylindrical in shape, which might, from a distance, have
been taken for dismounted cannon.

"There are our shells," said Herr Schultz.

"This time Max was obliged to acknowledge that they
resembled nothing he had ever seen before. They were
enormous tubes, six feet in length and three in diameter,
sheathed in lead in such a way as to fit into the rifling of
the gun, closed behind by a steel plate, and the point
finished off by a steel tip, supplied with a percussion
button.

Nothing in their appearance indicated the special
nature of these shells; though Max felt that in them
was contained some terrible element of destruction,
surpassing all that had ever before been made or
thought of.

"Can you not guess?" asked Herr Schultz, seeing that
his companion remained silent.

"Indeed, no, sir! Why should you want a shell so long and so heavy—in appearance at least ?"

"The appearance is deceitful," answered Herr Schultz ; "and there is no great difference in their weight to that of an ordinary shell of the same calibre. Come! I must tell you everything. A fusee shell of glass, encased in oak, charged with liquid carbonic acid by seventy atmospheres of interior pressure. The fall provokes the explosion of the case and the return of the liquid to a gaseous state. An enormous volume of carbonic acid gas rushes into the air, and a cold of a hundred degrees below zero seizes upon the surrounding atmosphere. Every living thing within a radius of thirty yards from the centre of the explosion is at once frozen and suffocated. I say thirty yards as the lowest calculation, but the action would really extend much farther, say to a hundred or a couple of hundred yards.

"Another capital thing about it is, that the carbonic acid gas, remaining a very long time near the ground, by reason of its weight, being greater than that of air, will preserve the dangerous properties of the zone for many hours after the first explosion, so that any creature which may attempt to enter or pass through it, must infallibly perish. The effect of that shot will be both instantaneous and lasting. Besides, with my plan, there will be no wounded, only dead !"

Herr Schultz displayed manifest pleasure in exhibiting the merits of his invention. His good humour had returned, he was flushed with pride, and his teeth gleamed.

"You are to imagine," he resumed, "a sufficient number of my pieces of ordnance directed against a besieged town. Supposing one sufficient for the destruction of a place of two acres and a half in extent, then, for a town of two thousand five hundred acres, we must have a hundred batteries, each consisting of ten suitable guns. Now, let us suppose all our guns in position, the weather calm and favourable, the general signal given by an electric wire. In a minute there would not be a single living being remaining in an extent of two thousand five hundred acres! The town would be submerged in a regular ocean of carbonic acid gas! The idea occurred to me last year on reading the medical report of the accidental death of a little miner in the Albrecht pit. I had the first inspiration at Naples, when I visited the Dog Grotto.[1] But that last fact was needed to put the finishing stroke to my thought. You comprehend the principle, do you not? An artificial

---

[1] The Grotto del Cano, in the neighbourhood of Naples, borrows its name from the curious property its atmosphere possesses of suffocating a dog, or any small four-legged animal, without doing any harm to a man standing upright—this is owing to a layer of about two feet of carbonic acid gas, which is kept by its specific weight close to the ground.

ocean of pure carbonic acid! Now, the proportion of a fifth of this gas would be sufficient to render the air unbreathable."

Max did not utter a word. He was regularly struck dumb. Herr Schultz felt his triumph so keenly, that he did not wish to take advantage of it.

"There is only one detail which troubles me," said he.

"And what can that be?" asked Max.

"That I have not succeeded in suppressing the sound of the explosion. It makes my gun too much like a common cannon. Just think of what it would be if I could manage to have a silent shot. Sudden death comes noiselessly upon a hundred thousand men at once, on some calm and serene night!"

The enchanting prospect thus called up, threw Herr Schultz into a brown study. From this reverie, which was but a deep immersion in a bath of self-love, he was aroused by Max observing—

"Very good, sir, very good! but a thousand guns of this description mean time and money."

"Money? we are overflowing with it! Time? Time is ours!"

And indeed this German, the last of his school, believed what he said.

"Well," replied Max, "your shell loaded with carbonic acid is not perfectly new after all, for it is derived from those suffocating projectiles which have been known for many years; but that it may be eminently destructive, I do not deny.   Only——"

"Only?"

"It is light for its size, and if it is ever projected thirty miles——"

"It is only made to go six," answered Herr Schultz, smiling.   "But," he added, pointing to another shell, "here is one of steel. This fellow is full, and contains a hundred little guns, symmetrically arranged, fitted one into the other, like the parts of a telescope.   Having been fired as projectiles, they will become cannon to vomit forth in their turn little shells loaded with incendiary matter. It will be a whole battery hurled through space, to carry flame and death into a town by covering it with a shower of inextinguishable fire! This has the requisite weight to go the thirty miles of which I spoke.   In a short time a trial of it will be made in such a way that unbelievers may go if they like and handle the hundred thousand corpses which it will have stretched on the ground!"

Here the dominoes gleamed so intolerably in Herr Schultz's mouth, that Max felt a strong desire to smash in a dozen or so of them, but contained himself. He had not yet heard all.

Herr Schultz resumed—

" I have said that a decisive experiment is shortly to be made."

" How ? Where ?" cried Max.

" How ? With one of these shells, which thrown by my gun from the platform, will cross the Cascade mountains. Where ? There exists a city, separated from us by at most thirty miles, upon whose inhabitants it will come like a thunder-clap, for even if they expected it, they could not ward it off, or escape the startling effects. This is now the 5th of September. Well,. on the 13th, at a quarter before midnight, Frankville will disappear from off American soil ! The burning of Sodom will be rivalled. Professor Schultz, in his turn, will let loose the fires of Heaven !"

At this unexpected declaration Max felt the blood curdle in his veins. Fortunately Herr Schultz did not perceive his agitation.

" Now you see," he continued in an easy tone, " we act just contrary to the founders of Frankville. We search for the secret of abridging the lives of men, whilst they seek to lengthen them. However, everything has an object in nature, and Dr. Sarrasin, by founding that isolated city, has, without suspecting it, placed a most magnificent field of experiments within my reach."

Max could scarcely believe his ears.

" But," said he, and the involuntary tremor in his voice

attracted for a moment the attention of the King of Steel, "the inhabitants of Frankville have done nothing to you, sir. You have not, so far as I know, any reason for picking a quarrel with them."

"My dear fellow," replied Herr Schultz, "in your brain, though well organised in other respects, there is a fund of Celtic ideas, which would do you much injury were you to live long enough! Right—Good—Evil are purely relative, and quite conventional words. Nothing is positive but the grand laws of nature. The law of competition has the same claim as that of gravitation. It is folly to resist, while to submit and follow in the way it points out, is only wise and reasonable, and therefore I mean to destroy Doctor Sarrasin's city. Thanks to my cannon, my fifty thousand Germans will easily make an end of the hundred thousand dreamers over there, who now constitute a group condemned to perish."

Seeing that an attempt to argue with Herr Schultz would be useless, Max did not try to soften him.

The two then left the shell chamber, closed the secret doors, and returned to the dining-room.

In the coolest, most natural way, the professor again lifted his tankard to his lips, touched a bell, called for a pipe in the place of the one he had broken, and then addressing the footman—

"Are Arminius and Sigimer there?" he asked.

"Yes, sir."

"Tell them to remain within call."

When the servant had left the room, the King of Steel turned to Max and looked him full in the face.

The latter's eyes did not quail before that look of almost metallic hardness.

"You mean really," said he, "to put your project into execution ?"

"Really. I know the situation and the latitude and longitude of Frankville to the tenth of a second, and on the 13th of September, at a quarter before midnight, it will cease to be."

" Perhaps you ought to have kept this plan an absolute secret."

" My dear fellow," answered Herr Schultz, " decidedly your mind never would become logical. This makes me regret the less that you must die young."

At these words Max started up.

"Is it possible you do not understand," added Herr Schultz, coldly, " that I never speak of my plans but before those who cannot repeat them ?"

The bell rang. Arminius and Sigimer, two giants, appeared at the door.

"You wished to know my secret," said Herr Schultz, "you do know it. Nothing remains for you now but to die !"

Max did not reply.

"You are too intelligent," resumed Herr Schultz, "to suppose that I can let you live, now that you know all about my plans. That would be an act of unpardonable carelessness ; that would be illogical. The greatness of my aim forbids me to compromise its success for the consideration of a relative value so trifling as the life of a man— even of such a man as you, my dear fellow, whose good cerebral organisation I most particularly esteem. Now I truly regret that a little movement of self-love should have carried me away and placed me under the necessity of suppressing you. But you must understand that in the face of the interests to which I have devoted myself, there can be no question of sentiment. I may as well tell you now, that it was for having penetrated my secret that your predecessor met his death, and not by an explosion of dynamite ! The rule is strict, it must be inflexible ! I can alter nothing."

Max looked at Herr Schultz. He understood by the sound of his voice, by the unrelenting obstinacy of that. bald head that he was lost. He did not give himself the trouble of uttering a word of protest.

"When, and by what death shall I die ?" he merely asked.

"Don't be uneasy about that," replied Herr Schultz, composedly. "You will die ; but suffering will be spared you. You will not wake up some morning. That is all."

At a sign from the King of Steel, Max found himself led away, and shut into his room, the door of which was guarded by the two giants.

But when he found himself alone, he thought with a shudder of agony and rage of the doctor, his relations, compatriots, all those whom he loved.

"The death which awaits me is nothing," he said to himself. "But how am I to avert the danger which threatens them ?"

CHAPTER IX.

P. P. C.

THE situation was indeed serious. What could pooɪ
Max do, he whose hours were already numbered, and
whose last night might have come with the setting
sun.

He did not sleep for an instant, not from the dread of
never awaking, as Herr Schultz had said, but because his
heart was too full of thoughts of Frankville and of the
impending catastrophe.

"What shall I attempt?" he thought to himself. "To
destroy that gun? Blow up the tower it stands on? How
could I manage it? Escape! Escape? when my room is
guarded by a couple of giants? And then suppose I could
get away from Stahlstadt before the 13th of September,
how could I help them? To be sure, if not our beloved
city, I might at least save the inhabitants. I might fly to
them shouting "Escape! escape without delay! You are

in danger of perishing by fire and steel! Fly all of you
for your lives!"

Then Max's thoughts passed into another channel.

"That villain Schultz!" he thought. "Even admitting
that he has exaggerated the destructive effects of his shell,
and that he cannot really fire the whole town, it is very
certain that with a single shot he can burn a considerable
part! It's a frightful machine he has invented, and notwithstanding the distance between the two towns, it will
easily send the projectile over it! The speed, too, must be
twenty times superior to any hitherto obtained. Something
like ten thousand yards, or nine miles a second! It's
actually a third of the speed of the earth in its orbit! Is
it possible? Oh, if only that horrible gun would blow up
at the first shot! But there is no hope of that, for the
metal of which it is made will stand anything. How
exactly the wretch knows the position of Frankville!
Without going out of his den, he can point his cannon with
mathematical precision, and, as he said, the shell will un-
doubtedly fall in the very heart of the city! How can
the unhappy inhabitants be warned?"

Max had not closed an eyelid when day dawned. He
then rose from the bed, on which he had tossed in feverish
restlessness. "Come," he said to himself, "it will be for
another night. As this executioner means to spare me
suffering, he no doubt will wait till sleep, getting the better

of my anxiety, has overpowered me. And then! What
sort of death can he have in store for me? Does he think
of killing me with some decoction of prussic acid whilst I
sleep? Will he introduce some of that carbonic acid gas,
which he has at his command, into my room? Will he
not rather use it in a liquid form, such as he has in his glass
shells, when its sudden return to a gaseous state produces
a hundred degrees of frost? And the next day, instead of
'me,' instead of this strong, well-constituted body, so full
of life, there will be nothing but a dried, frozen, shrivelled
mummy! Oh, the savage! Well, well, if it must be so,
let my heart be frozen and my life wither away in that
unbearable atmosphere, if only my friends, Doctor Sarrasin,
his family, Jeannette—my little Jeannette—may be saved!
But to effect that I must escape. Well, escape I
will!"

As he uttered these words, Max, though he believed
himself locked into his room, instinctively laid his hand on
the handle of the door.

To his great surprise it opened, and he went down as
usual, and out into the garden, where he was accustomed
to walk.

"Ah," he thought, "I am a prisoner in the Central Block,
though not in my room. That's something in my favour!"

However, no sooner was Max outside, than he saw that,
though apparently free, he in reality could not make a step

without being escorted by the two personages who answered
to the historic, or rather pre-historic, names of Arminius
and Sigimer.

He had often wondered, when he met them about the
place, what could be the duty of those two huge men in
grey cloaks, with their bull necks, herculean muscles, dark
red faces, bristling with thick moustaches and bushy
whiskers.

He now knew what that duty was. They were the
executioners of Herr Schultz's darkest deeds, who for the
present were acting as his body-guard !

These two giants never let him out of their sight, lying
at the door of his room, and dogging his steps when he
walked in the park. The formidable array of revolvers
and daggers which each carried in his belt rendered
hopeless any attempt to escape from them.

With all this, they were as dumb as fish.

Max tried, in a diplomatic way, to get up a conversation
with them, but only received a ferocious glare in reply.
Even the offer of a glass of beer, which he had some
reason to suppose irresistible, was made in vain. After
observing them for fifteen hours, he discovered that they
had one weakness, only one—a pipe, which they took the
liberty of smoking close at his heels. This single weakness
Max determined to turn to account. How, he did not
know, he could not even imagine, but he had vowed to

escape, and nothing should be neglected that could in any way assist him.

Time was pressing. What was to be done?

At the least sign of rebellion or flight, Max was sure of receiving a couple of bullets in his head. Even supposing they missed, he was still in the centre of a triple fortified line, guarded by a triple row of sentinels.

According to his custom, the former pupil of the Central School correctly put the situation in the form of a mathematical problem.

"Given, a man guarded by two unscrupulous ruffians, individually stronger than he, and armed to the teeth. The man must first escape the vigilance of these warders. This done, he must get out of a fortified place, all the entrances to which are strictly watched."

Max pondered this double question a hundred times, but always came to the conclusion "Which is impossible." However, the gravity of his situation seemed to sharpen all his faculties of invention. Whether chance alone gave the finishing touch or not would be difficult to say.

It happened that the next day, as Max was walking in the park, his eyes fell on a shrub, the appearance of which instantly attracted him.

It was a dull-looking herbaceous plant, its leaves alternately oval, pointed and double, with great red bell-shaped monopetalous flowers hanging by auxiliary stalks.

Max had merely studied botany as an amateur, but it immediately occurred to him that this shrub had the characteristics of one of the order Solanaceæ.

Quite at a venture, he gathered a leaf and slightly chewed it as he pursued his walk. He was not mistaken. A feeling of heaviness in his limbs, accompanied by a sensation of nausea, soon convinced him that he had close at hand a natural laboratory of bella-donna, that is to say, the most active of all narcotics.

He strolled on until he reached a small artificial lake, which stretched away to the southern end of the park, and supplied a cascade, which, by the bye, was evidently copied from that in the Bois de Boulogne.

" Where does the water of that cascade go to ? " thought Max.

It first flowed into the bed of a little river, which, after describing various turns and bends, finally disappeared at the limits of the park.

There was evidently an outlet, and, to all appearance, the river escaped by filling one of the subterranean channels which watered the plain beyond Stahlstadt.

In this Max saw a gate of egress. It was certainly not a carriage way, but it was an opening.

' And suppose the channel is barred by an iron grating ! " objected the voice of prudence.

" Nothing venture nothing have ! Files weren't made to

gnaw away corks, and there are capital files in the laboratory!" so answered another ironical voice, one that prompted daring resolves.

In two minutes Max's determination was made. An idea—as it may be called—had darted into his mind, one that perhaps could not after all be carried out, but which he would attempt, if death did not first overtake him.

He sauntered back towards the shrub with red flowers, and gathered two or three leaves in such a way that his guards could not fail to see him.

Then, returning to his room, he quite openly dried these leaves before the fire, rubbed them in his hands to crush them, and mixed them with his tobacco.

During the six following days, Max, to his extreme surprise, woke up quite well every morning. Had Herr Schultz, whom he had not again seen and never met in his walks—had he given up his plan of making away with him ? No, it was not likely, any more than he would relinquish that of destroying Doctor Sarrasin's city.

Max made use of this permission to live, and every day renewed his manœuvre. He took care, of course, never to smoke the bella-donna himself, and therefore kept two packets of tobacco, one for his personal use, the other for daily show. His object was simply to arouse the curiosity of Arminius and Sigimer. Confirmed smokers, such as these two ruffians, were sure soon to notice the shrub from which he took the leaves, imitate the operation, and try how they liked the mixture.

This supposition was correct, and the result proved equal to his anticipations.

On the sixth day, the eve of the fatal 13th of September, Max, as he glanced carelessly behind him, had the satisfaction of seeing his guards collect a little store of the green leaves.

An hour later, he observed that they were drying them at the fire, rubbing them in their great horny hands, and mixing them with their tobacco. They seemed already licking their lips in anticipation.

Was it Max's intention merely to stupefy Arminius and Sigimer? No, that was not sufficient. Eluding their vigilance he had still to pass down that stream, even if it should prove to be miles in length. But he had arranged his plan. It was true, there were nine chances in ten that he would perish; but as he was already condemned to death, that did not much matter.

Evening came, with it the supper hour, afterwards a walk. The inseparable trio took the way into the park.

Without hesitating, without losing a minute, Max proceeded straight towards a building, standing alone, and which was no other than the workshop where all the models were made. He sat down on a bench outside, filled his pipe, and began to smoke.

Arminius and Sigimer, who had their pipes all ready, sat down on a neighbouring seat and soon were puffing away.

The effects of the narcotic were not long in becoming visible.

: Before five minutes had passed, the two clumsy giants were yawning and stretching like bears in a cage. Their eyes grew dim, a dull sound was in their ears ; their complexions changed from red to purple, their arms fell useless at their sides, their heads dropped on their breasts.

The pipes slipped to the ground.

Then followed loud snoring, mingled with the twittering of the birds, who lived all the year round in the perpetual summer of the Stahlstadt park.

Now was Max's time. His impatience may be imagined, when it is remembered that in the next night, at a quarter before midnight, Frankville, having been sentenced by Herr Schultz, would cease to exist.

He darted into the workshop. It was a large building, a perfect museum of models. Hydraulic machines, locomotives, steam engines, portable engines, suction pumps, boring machines, ships, ship machinery, in fact, the masterpieces would be too numerous to mention. It was a collection of models in wood of everything made in the Schultz manufactory since its foundation, and you may be sure that many cannon, torpedoes, and shells were amongst them.

The night was dark, and favourable to the young Alsaoian's daring project. Besides accomplishing his escape he hoped to destroy the Stahlstadt Model Museum.

How he longed to annihilate that huge Bull Tower, with its destructive cannon and all it contained ; but it was useless to think of that.

Max's first care was to seize a little steel saw, fit for filing iron, which was hanging from a tool rack, and slip it into his pocket. Then taking a match from his box, he struck it, set fire to a heap of drawings and slight fir-wood models, and rushed out.

The fire spreading among all these inflammable materials increased with great rapidity, and flames speedily burst forth from every part of the building. The alarm-bell rang, the electric wire carried the news to every quarter of Stahlstadt, peals sounded, and firemen and engines hastened from all directions.

At the same moment Herr Schultz, whose presence was well calculated to encourage the workers, made his appearance.

In a very few minutes, the boilers were under pressure and the powerful pumps at work. But in spite of the deluges of water which fell on the walls and roofs, the fire gained force, and it was soon evident that all hope of mastering it must be given up. It was a grand and terrible spectacle.

Crouched in a corner, Max never lost sight of Herr Schultz, who cheered on his men as if assaulting a town. There was no necessity for giving a further helping hand to the fire. The Museum, standing as it did, alone in the park, would soon be entirely consumed.

Herr Schultz, seeing that the building itself could not possibly be saved, suddenly shouted out—

"Ten thousand dollars to whoever will save model, number 3175, from the glass case in the centre!"

This was the very mould of Schultz's famous cannon, and he valued it above all other things in the Museum.

To reach it, however, a person would be compelled to make his way through a deluge of sparks and falling wood, and an unbreathable atmosphere of dense black smoke. It was ten to one that he would escape with his life. Notwithstanding, therefore, the magnificence of Herr Schultz's offer, no one answered to his appeal.

At last a man presented himself.

It was Max.

" I will go," said he.

'You !" exclaimed Herr Schultz.

'Yes, I !"

"It won't save you from the sentence of death pronounced against you, so don't imagine it !"

"I do not propose to avoid that, but to snatch your precious model from destruction."

"Go then," answered Herr Schultz, "and I swear that if you succeed, the ten thousand dollars shall be faithfully made over to your heirs."

"I will depend on you for that," returned Max.

Several of the Galibert apparatus were brought to him ; they were always at hand in case of fire, as they enabled men to venture into the densest smoke. Max had already made use of one when he tried to save from death dame Bauer's boy, poor little Carl.

One of these was soon filled with air and placed on his back. He put the pincers on his nose, took the tube in his mouth, and darted into the smoke.

"At last!" said he. "This air will last for a quarter of an hour! Heaven grant that may be time enough!"

As may be imagined, Max had not the slightest intention of endeavouring to save Schultz's cannon model. His life every moment in dire peril, he made his way across the smoke-filled hall, amidst a shower of blazing brands and charred beams. Mercifully none of them touched him, and just as the roof fell in with a fearful crash, Max escaped at the opposite side of the building.

To fly towards the stream, run along its banks till he reached the unknown opening and plunge in, was the work of only a few seconds.

The rapid current swept him along in a depth of seven or eight feet. He had no need to guide himself, for the water bore him as straight as if he had held Ariadne's clue.

He soon found that he had entered a narrow channel, a sort of pipe, quite filled by the overflow of the river.

"What can be the length of this tunnel?" thought Max. "Everything depends on that! If I do not pass through it in a quarter of an hour, the air will fail and I am lost!"

He maintained his coolness and presence of mind. Ten minutes passed, when suddenly he was driven up against some obstacle.

This was an iron grating on hinges, barring the way down the tunnel.

"This is what I feared!" thought Max simply.

Without losing a moment, he took the saw from his pocket, and set to work on the bolt of the staple.

Five minutes labour did not loosen it, the grating remained obstinately closed. Already Max breathed with difficulty. There came a buzzing in his ears, the blood mounted in his head, he felt he would soon lose consciousness.

He endeavoured, however, to make the most of the small quantity of air remaining, by taking breath as seldom as possible! Though half sawn through, the bolt would not yield!

At that moment the saw slipped from his hands.

"Surely God himself cannot be against me!" was his thought.

And grasping the grating with both hands, he shook it with the despairing energy given by the instinct of self-preservation.

The grating opened. The bolt had given way, and the current carried onwards the daring Alsacian, nearly suffocated, yet still feebly struggling, as he inhaled the last particles of air in the reservoir!

*   *   *   *   *   *

The next day, when Herr Schultz's men ventured into the ruins left by the fire, they searched in vain among all the débris, and still smouldering cinders for any trace of human remains. It was evident that the brave workman had perished.

His daring act astonished none of his friends who had known him in the different workshops.

The precious model was not saved, but the man who was acquainted with the secrets of the Steel King was dead.

"Heaven is witness that I wished to spare him all suffering," said Herr Schultz to himself, in his usual serene fashion. "At any rate, as I know not his heirs, I am saved ten thousand dollars!"

Such was the only funeral oration pronounced by the philosophical professor over the supposed grave of our young Alsacian!

CHAPTER X.

AN ARTICLE FROM 'UNSERE CENTURIE,' A GERMAN REVIEW.

A MONTH before the period at which the events we have just related occurred, a review, in a salmon-coloured wrapper, entitled " Our Century," published the following article on the subject of Frankville, an article which was particularly relished by the fastidious people of the German Empire, perhaps, because it only studied that city from a purely material point of view :

"We have already given our readers an account of the extraordinary phenomenon which has been produced on the western coast of the United States. The great American republic, owing to the large proportion of emigrants included in its population, has for long accustomed the world to a succession of surprises ; but the last, and certainly the most singular, is that of a city named Frankville. Though the very idea of it did not exist five years ago, it is now flourishing, and in the highest degree of prosperity.

"This marvellous city has risen as if by enchantment on the balmy shores of the Pacific. We will not inquire whether it is true (as we are assured) that the first plan and idea of this enterprise is due to a Frenchman, Doctor Sarrasin. The thing is possible, as this doctor may boast a distant relationship with our illustrious King of Steel. We may also say in passing, it is rumoured that a considerable inheritance, which should properly have come to Herr Schultz, has had something to do with the founding of Frankville. Wherever any good springs up in the world, we may be certain that it is from German seed; this is a truth we are proud of stating whenever an opportunity offers. But, however that may be, we now wish to give our readers some precise and authentic details on the subject of the spontaneous vegetation of a model city.

"It is useless to look for its name on the map. Even the great atlas in three hunderd and seventy-eight folio volumes, by our eminent Tuchtigmann, in which every thicket and clump of trees in the old and new world are put in with such exactitude, even this noble monument to geographical science, designed for the use of sharpshooters, does not bear the least trace of Frankville.

The place where the new city now **stands** was five years

ago a complete desert. The exact spot lies 43° 11′ 3″ north latitude, and 124° 41′ 17″ west longitude.

" It will be seen that this is on the shores of the Pacific Ocean, and at the foot of the secondary chain of the Rocky Mountains, called the Cascade Mountains, sixty miles to the north of White Cape, Oregon State, North America.

"This most advantageous site has been carefully sought ₃nd chosen from among a number of others. The prominent reasons for its adoption are the temperate climate of the northern hemisphere, which has always been at the head of terrestrial civilisation ; its position, in the middle of a federative republic, and in a still new State, which has allowed it to secure its independence, and rights similar to those possessed by the principality of Monaco in Europe, on the condition that after a certain number of years it would enter the Union. Its situation on the Ocean, which is becoming more and more the great highway of the globe ; the varied, fertile, and salubrious nature of the soil ; the proximity of a chain of mountains, sheltering it from the north, south, and east winds, leaving to the fresh Pacific breeze the care of renovating the atmosphere of the city ; the possession of a little river, whose fresh, sweet, clear water, oxygenated by repeated falls, and by the rapidity of its course, arrives perfectly pure at the sea ; lastly, a natural port, formed by a long curved promontory, which may easily be enlarged by moles.

"A few secondary advantages may be mentioned, such as the proximity of fine marble and stone quarries, bearings of kaolin, and even traces of auriferous ore. In fact, this last detail was almost the cause of the site being given up, for the founders of the town feared that the gold fever might come in the way of their plans. Fortunately, however, the nuggets were found to be small and not numerous.

"The choice of a territory, although determined upon after serious and close study, took but a few days, and was not made the subject of a special expedition. Science is now so far advanced that, without leaving his study, a man may gather exact and particular information about the most distant regions.

"This point decided, two commissioners of the organisation committee took the first boat from Liverpool, arrived in eleven days at New York, in seven more at San Francisco, where they chartered a steamer, which in ten hours landed them on the proposed site.

"To come to terms with the legislature of Oregon, to obtain a grant of twelve miles of land on the shores of the sea on the crest of the Cascade Mountains, to indemnify with a few millions of dollars the half-dozen planters who had some real or supposed rights on the ground, all this business did not take more than a month.

"By January 1872, the territory was already surveyed,

measured, laid out, and an army of twenty thousand Chinese coolies, under the direction of five hundred overseers and European engineers, were hard at work. Placards posted up all over the State of California, an advertisement van permanently attached to the rapid train, which starts every morning from San Francisco to traverse the American continent, and a daily article in the twenty-three newspapers of that town, were sufficient to ensure the recruiting of the labourers. It was not even found necessary to resort to the expedient of publishing on a grand scale, by means of gigantic letters sculptured on the peaks of the Rocky Mountains, that men were wanted. It must be said that the influx of Chinese coolies into western America had just at this time caused much perturbation in the labour market. Several States had, in the interest of their own population, actually expelled these unfortunate people *en masse.* The building of Frankville came just in time to save them from perishing. Their wages, fixed at a dollar a day, were not to be paid them until the works were finished, and their rations were distributed by the municipal administration. Thus all the disorder and shameful speculations, which so often attend any great displacement of population, were avoided. The wages were deposited every week, in the presence of delegates, in the great Bank at San Francisco, and every coolie was warned that when he drew it out, he was not to return. This precaution was absolutely necessary to get rid of a yellow population, which would otherwise have infallibly lowered the tone and standard of the new city. The founders having, besides, reserved the right of granting or refusing permission to live there, the application of this measure was comparatively easy.

" The first great enterprise was the establishment of a branch railway, connecting the territory of the new town with the trunk of the Pacific Railroad, and running to Sacramento. These works, and those of the harbour, were pushed on with extraordinary activity. In April, the first train, direct from New York, brought to the Frankville terminus the members of the committee, who, until this time, had remained in Europe.

" In this interval, the general plan of the town, the details of habitations and public monuments had been stopped.

" This was not from want of materials ; from the very first, American industry had hastened to load the quays of Frankville with every imaginable requisite for building. It was merely the difficulty of choice. The founders at last decided that the freestone should be reserved for national edifices and general ornamenation, and that all houses should be built of brick. Not, it must be understood, of common roughly-moulded, half-baked bricks, but light, well-shaped ones, regular in size, weight, and density, and pierced from end to end with a series of cylindrical and parallel holes.　These bricks, when placed together, allowed the air to circulate freely throughout the walls of the building.[1]　This arrangement had at the same time the valuable effect of deadening sounds, and giving complete independence to each apartment.

"The committee did not wish to impose a model on the builders.　They were averse to a wearisome and insipid uniformity, and merely gave a certain number of fixed rules, to which the architects were bound to adhere.

"1st.—Each house to stand alone in a plot of ground planted with trees, grass, and flowers, and to be inhabited by a single family.

"2nd.—No house to be more than two stories high : air and light must not be monopolised by some, to the detriment of others.

"3rd.—Every house must be set back ten yards from the road, and divided from it by a breast-high railing.　The space between the building and the railing must be laid out as a garden.

"4th.—The walls to be built of the patent tubular bricks, similar to the model.　All ornamentation to be left to the taste of the architect.

"5th.—The roofs to be in terraces, slightly inclined from the four sides, covered with bitumen, surrounded by a

---

[1] These plans, as well as the general idea, are borrowed from Doctor Benjamin Ward Richardson, Member of the Royal Society of London.

balustrade high enough to render accidents impossible, and proper canals made for the passing off of rain-water.

"6th.—All the houses must be built on a vaulted foundation, open on each side, and thus forming under the ground-floor a subsoil of aeration, as well as a hall. All water-pipes must be exposed, running up the central pillar, in such a way that it may be always easy to ascertain their state, and in case of fire, to be able to obtain the necessary water immediately. The floor of this hall, rising about three inches above the level of the road, must be properly gravelled. A door and a special staircase will place it in direct communication with the kitchens and offices, so that all household transactions may go on without offending either the eyes or the nose.

"7th.—The kitchens and offices will, contrary to the usual custom, be placed in the upper story, and in communication with the terrace. A lift, moved by mechanical force, which, like artificial light and water, will be supplied at reduced prices to the inhabitants, will easily convey all loads to this level.

"8th.—The plan of the rooms is left to individual taste. But two dangerous elements of illness, regular nests of miasma and laboratories of poison, are to be strictly excluded—carpets and painted papers. The floors, beautifully inlaid with valuable woods by clever workmen, would be quite wasted were they hidden under a woollen cloth of

doubtful cleanliness. The walls, lined with polished
bricks, present the brilliancy and variety of the inner apartments of Pompeii, with a luxury of colour, which painted
paper, charged with its thousand subtile poisons, could
never reach. They are washed as windows are washed,
and rubbed like ceilings and floors. Not even a germ of
anything harmful can be harboured there.

" 9th.—Each bedroom is distinct from the dressing-room.
It cannot be too much recommended that the former
apartment, where a third of a man's life is passed, should
be the largest, the most airy, and at the same time the
most simple. It must only be used for sleep; four chairs,
an iron bedstead, supplied with two frequently-beaten
mattresses, is the only necessary furniture. Eider-down
quilts and heavy coverlets, powerful allies of epidemics,
are excluded as a matter of course. Good woollen cover-
ings, light and warm, and easily washed, replace them
well. Though curtains and draperies are not absolutely
forbidden, it is recommended that, if used, they should be
made of washing materials.

" 10th.—Each room may be warmed according to fancy
by wood or coal; but to every chimney is a corresponding
opening to the outer air. The smoke, instead of issuing
through the roof, is led away by subterranean pipes to
special furnaces, established, outside the town, at the back
of the houses, at the rate of a furnace to every two

hundred inhabitants. There it is deprived of the particles of carbon which it bears, and is discharged in a colourless state into the air, at a height of thirty-five yards. Such are the ten rules imposed on the building of each particular house.

"The general arrangements are no less carefully studied.

"The plan of the town is essentially simple and regular, the roads crossing at right angles, at equal distances, of a uniform width, planted with trees, and numbered.

"Some of the roads being wider, are then called boulevards or avenues, and leave on one side rails for tramways and metropolitan railways. Public gardens are numerous, and ornamented with fine copies of the masterpieces of sculpture, until the artists of Frankville shall have produced original pieces worthy to replace them.

"Every industry and trade is free.

"Any one wishing to have the right of living in Frankville must give good references, be fit to follow a useful or liberal profession in industry, science, or the arts, and must engage to keep the laws of the town. An idle life would not be tolerated there.

"There are already a large number of public edifices. The most important are the Cathedral, chapels, museums, libraries, schools, and gymnasiums, fitted up with the luxury and hygienic skill worthy of a great city.

"It is needless to say that from the age of four years all

children are obliged to follow physical and intellectual exercises, calculated to develope the brain and muscles. They are also accustomed to such strict cleanliness, that they consider a spot on their simple clothes quite a disgrace.

" Individual and collective cleanliness is the great idea of the founders of Frankville. To clean, clean unceasingly, so as to destroy the miasmas constantly emanating from a large community, such is the principal work of the central government. For this purpose, all the contents of the drains are led out of the town, condensed, and daily transferred to the fields.

" Water flows everywhere in abundance.

" The streets are paved with bituminated wood ; and the stone footpaths are as spotless as a courtyard in Holland. The provision markets are subject to strict surveillance, and any merchants who dare to speculate on the public health incur the severest penalties. The man who sells a bad egg, damaged meat, or a pint of adulterated milk, is simply treated as the poisoner he really is. This necessary and delicate office is confided to experienced men, who receive a special education for it. Their jurisdiction extends to the very laundries, which are on a large scale, provided with steam engines, artificial dryers, and, above all, with disinfecting-rooms. No body-linen is sent back to its owners without being thoroughly bleached, and special care is taken never to mix the washing of two families. This simple precaution is of great value. Hospitals are few in number, for the system of house nursing is general, and they are reserved for homeless strangers and exceptional cases. The idea of making the hospital larger than any other building, and of putting seven or eight hundred patients under one roof, so as to make a centre of infection, would not enter the head of the founders of this model city. Far from this, it is in theirs, as well as in the public interest, to isolate the sick as much as possible. This is the plan pursued in the houses, the hospitals being merely for the temporary accommodation of the most pressing cases.

"Twenty or thirty patients at most, each having a separate apartment, are put into these light barracks, which are built of fir-wood, and burnt regularly every year. They have, besides, the advantage of being easily carried from one part of the town to another as they are wanted, and, being all on one model, can be multiplied to any extent.

"Another ingenious institution is that of a body of experienced nurses, specially trained for the purpose, and always at the disposal of the public. These women, being carefully chosen, are most valuable and devoted aids to the doctors. They bring into the bosom of families that practical knowledge, so necessary and yet so often absent;

in the time of danger it is their mission to prevent the spread of the disease as well as to tend the sick.

"We should never finish were we to attempt to enumerate all the hygienic perfections inaugurated by the founders of this new town. On his arrival each citizen is presented with a small pamphlet, in which the most important principles of a life, regulated according to science, are set forth in clear and simple language.

"He is there told that the perfect equilibrium of all the functions is one of the necessities for health, that work and rest are equally indispensable, that fatigue is as necessary for the brain as for the muscles; that nine-tenths of the illnesses are owing to contagion transmitted by air and food. He cannot surround his dwelling and his person with too many sanitary precautions. To avoid the use of exciting poisons, to practise bodily exercises, to conscientiously perform every day some appointed duty, to drink pure water, to eat fresh meat and vegetables simply prepared, to sleep regularly seven or eight hours a night, such is the A B C of health.

"Beginning from the first principles laid down by the founders, we have been led on to speak of this singular city as already finished. It is indeed so; the first houses built, the others rose as if by magic. A man should have previously visited the far west in order to realise the wonderful change. The site that was a desert in the

month of January 1872, contained six thousand houses in
1873. In 1874 it possessed nine thousand, and all public
edifices complete.

" Speculation has certainly had its part in this unheard-of
success. The ground having cost nothing, the houses
could be sold or let at very moderate prices. There being
no taxes, the political independence of this isolated little
territory, its novelty, and the pleasant climate, all contributed to induce emigration. At the present time
Frankville contains nearly a hundred thousand inhabitants.

" But to us the most interesting part of it is that the
result of the sanitary experiment is conclusive.

" Whilst the annual mortality in the most favoured towns
of Europe or the New World has never been less than
three per cent., in Frankville for these five years the
average has been one and a half. Even this figure was
increased by a slight fever epidemic during the first
summer. That of the last year was only one and a
quarter. And a more important circumstance still, is that,
with but a few exceptions, all the deaths actually registered
were due to specific and hereditary affections. Accidental
illnesses have been at once infinitely rarer, and less
dangerous, than in any other great centre. As to epidemics, properly so called, nothing has been seen or heard
of them.

" It will be interesting to follow the development of this

attempt, and certainly curious to discover if the influence
of this scientific régime may not in the course of a genera-
tion, or more likely still, after several generations, weaken
hereditary and morbid predispositions.

" ' It is assuredly not too much to hope,' as one of the
founders has written, ' and if so what may not be the
grandeur of the result! Everybody living for ninety or a
hundred years, and then only dying of old age, as do the
greater number of animals and plants.'

" There is something enchanting in such a dream!
Nevertheless, if we may be allowed to express our sincere
opinion, we have but an indifferent belief in the actual
success of this experiment. We see in it an original and
probably fatal flaw, which is its being in the hands of a
committee in which the Latin element prevails, and from
which the German element has been systematically
excluded. That is a bad symptom. Since the world began
nothing durable has been made but by Germany, and
without her nothing perfect can be effected. The founders
of Frankville may clear the ground, and elucidate some
special points ; not, however, on this spot in America, but
on the borders of Syria, shall we one day see the true
model city arise."

CHAPTER XI.

AT DINNER WITH DOCTOR SARRASIN.

ON the 13th of September, although it wanted but a few hours to the time fixed on by Professor Schultz for the destruction of Frankville, neither the governor nor a single person among the inhabitants dreamed of the danger which threatened them.

Seven o'clock in the evening arrived.

Half buried in thick masses of oleander and tamarinds, the beautiful city lay at the foot of the Cascade Mountains, its marble quays gently caressed by the waves of the Pacific. The carefully watered roads, freshened by the breeze, presented a cheerful and animated spectacle. The trees which shaded them rustled softly. The velvet lawns were fresh and green. Brilliant beds of flowers exhaled their sweetness around the calm and smiling white houses. The air was warm and balmy, and the sky as blue as the sea, which glittered at the end of the long avenues.

A stranger arriving in the town would have been at once struck with the healthful look of the inhabitants and the activity in the streets.   The academies of painting, music, and sculpture, and the library, all in the same quarter, had just been closed.   Excellent public courses were given there to small sections, so that each pupil might get the full advantage of the lesson.   Among the crowds issuing from these places, and naturally causing some stoppage, not an exclamation of impatience, nor an angry look, was heard or seen.   The general aspect was one of calmness and satisfaction.

Not in the centre of the town, but on the shores of the Pacific, had Doctor Sarrasin built his house.   It had been among the first put up, and he had come immediately and established himself there with his wife and daughter Jeannette.

Octavius, the extempore millionaire, had chosen to remain in Paris ; but he had no longer Max for a mentor.

The two friends had almost lost sight of each other since the time when they lived together in King of Sicily Street.

When the doctor emigrated with his wife and daughter to the coast of Oregon, Otto was his own master.   He soon neglected college, where his father had wished him to continue his studies, and was in consequence plucked in the final examination, when his friend Max came out first.

Till then, poor Otto, who was incapable of managing for himself, had had Max for a guide. When the young Alsacian left, his companion directly began to see life in Paris. He passed the greater part of his time on the box of a four-in-hand coach, driving perpetually between the avenue Marigny, where he had rooms, and the various race-courses of the suburbs.

Otto Sarrasin, who, three months before, could scarcely manage to stick on a horse hired by the hour, had suddenly become deeply versed in the mysteries of hippology. His erudition was borrowed from an English groom who had entered his service, and who ruled him entirely, in consequence of the superiority of his special knowledge.

Interviews with tailors, saddlers, and bootmakers, occupied the mornings. His evenings were spent at the theatres and in the rooms of a flaming new club, just opened at the corner of Trouchet-Street, and chosen by Otto because the people he met there paid to his money a homage which his personal merits had not hitherto received.

The company seemed to him highly distinguished. A noticeable thing about it was that the handsomely framed list, hanging in the waiting-room, bore few but foreign names. Titles abounded, so that you might almost fancy yourself in the antechamber of an heraldic college. But on penetrating farther one might imagine oneself in a living ethnological exhibition. All the big noses and bilious complexions of the two hemispheres seemed to have met together there.

Otto Sarrasin reigned paramount among these worthies. His words were quoted, his cravats copied, his opinions accepted as articles of faith. And intoxicated with this incense of flattery, he never found out that he regularly lost money at play and the races. Perhaps certain members of the club, in their Oriental capacity, thought that they had some rights on the Begum's heritage. At any rate, they were able to gradually draw it into their pockets by a slow though continued process.

In this new life the ties which bound Otto to Max Bruckmann were soon loosened. At last, the two chums only exchanged letters at long intervals. What could there be in common between the eager hard-working man, solely occupied with bringing his intellect to the highest point of culture and strength, and the idle youth, puffed up with his riches, his thoughts only filled with club and stable gossip.

We know how Max left Paris, first to keep a watch on Herr Schultz, who had just founded Stahlstadt, the rival to Frankville, and then actually to enter the service of the King of Steel.

For two years Otto led his useless and dissipated life. Then a weariness of these hollow and worthless pleasures seized him, and one fine day, after having wasted so millions of francs, he rejoined his father, thus escaping from moral and physical ruin. At the present time he was living in the doctor's house in Frankville.

His sister Jeannette was now a lovely girl of nineteen, to whose French grace her four years' stay in the new country had added all the good American qualities. Her mother said sometimes that before having her so completely to herself, she had never felt the charm of perfect intimacy.

As to Madame Sarrasin, since the return of her prodigal son, the child of her hopes, she was as completely happy as any one can be here below, for she associated herself with all the good her husband could and did do with his immense fortune.

On the evening of which we have spoken, Doctor Sarrasin had invited to dinner two of his most intimate friends, Colonel Hendon, an old hero of the War of Secession, who had left an arm at Pittsburg, and an ear at Sevenoaks, but who could hold his own with any one at a game of chess ; and Monsieur Lentz, General Director of Instruction in the new city.

The conversation turned on the plans for the administration of the town, the results already obtained in the public establishments of all sorts, institutions, hospitals, mutual aid societies.

M. Lentz, according to the doctor's programme, in which

religious teaching was not forgotten, had founded several elementary schools, where the cares of the master tended to develope the mind of the child by submitting it to a sort of intellectual gymnastic exercise, adjusted so as to follow the natural bent of its faculties. It was taught to love a science before being crammed with it, avoiding that knowledge which, says Montaigne, "floats on the surface of the brain," without penetrating the understanding, or rendering its possessor either wiser or better. Later, a well-prepared intellect can of itself choose its path and follow it with profit.

The principles of health took a first place in this well-ordered education.

Man should have equal command both of his mind and, body. If one fails him he suffers for it, and the mind especially, if unsupported by the body, would soon give way.

Frankville had now reached the highest degree of intellectual as well as temporal prosperity. In its congress were collected all the illustrious and learned men of the two worlds. Artists, painters, sculptors, musicians, attracted by the reputation of this city, crowded to it. All the young people of Frankville, who promised some day to illuminate this corner of America, studied under these masters. This new Athens of French origin was on the way to become the first of cities. A good military as well

CHAPTER XII.

THE COUNCIL.

THE hatred which the King of Steel bore to Doctor Sarrasin's work was no secret. Every one knew that his was a rival city. But no one would have believed him capable of attacking a peaceful town, and endeavouring to destroy it at a blow. The article in the *New York Herald* was, however, positive on the point. The correspondents of that provincial journal had penetrated Herr Schultz's designs, and, as they said, there was not an hour to spare !

The worthy doctor was confounded. Like all honest-hearted men, he refused as long as he could to believe in the evil designs of others. It seemed to him impossible that a human being could be so wicked as to wish to destroy without sufficient reason, and from simple malice, a city, which was in a certain sense the common property of mankind.

"Just think that our average mortality will this year be only one and a quarter in every hundred!" he exclaimed, naïvely; "that there is not a boy of ten years old who does not know how to read ; that not a murder or theft has been committed since the foundation of Frankville! And these barbarians want to destroy this successful experiment at its very beginning! No ; I cannot believe that a chemist, a savant, were he a hundred times a German, could be capable of such atrocity!"

They were compelled, however, to trust to the evidence of a paper thoroughly devoted to their undertaking, and act without delay. The first moment of dismay passed, Doctor Sarrasin regaining the command of his feelings, thus addressed his friends—

"Gentlemen, you are members of the Civic Council, and it is your duty as well as mine to take all necessary measures for the safety of the town. What ought we to do first?"

"Is there no possibility of arranging matters?" said M. Lentz. "Can we not honourably avoid war?"

"That is impossible," replied Otto. "Herr Schultz evidently will have it at any price. His hate will not allow him to come to terms!"

"Very well!" exclaimed the doctor; "we shall be ready to receive him. Do you think, colonel, that any-thing can resist the cannons of Stahlstadt?"

"Any human force can be efficaciously combatted by another human force," answered Colonel Hendon; "but we need not think of defending ourselves by the same means and the same arms which Herr Schultz will use to attack us. The construction of engines of war, capable of opposing his, would take a long time to make, and I do not know, besides, if we should succeed in fabricating them, since we have not special workshops. I can only see one chance of safety, that of preventing the enemy from reaching us, and rendering an investment impossible."

"I will go immediately and convoke the Council," said Doctor Sarrasin; and he led his guests into his study.

It was a simply furnished room, three sides being covered with shelves, loaded with books, whilst the fourth presented, below several pictures and curiosities, a row of numbered openings, similar to ear-trumpets.

"Thanks to the telephone," said he, "we can hold a council in Frankville, whilst every one remains at home."

The doctor touched a warning-bell, which instantaneously communicated with the houses of all the members. In less than three minutes, the word "present" brought successively by each wire, announced that the Council was sitting.

The doctor placed himself before the mouthpiece, rung the bell, and said—

"The meeting is open. My honourable friend, Colonel

Hendon, will speak, to make a communication of the deepest importance."

The colonel, in his turn, placed himself before the telephone, and, after reading the article from the *New York Herald*, he proposed that immediate measures should be taken to impede the advance of the enemy.

He had scarcely concluded when number Six put the question—

"Does the colonel believe a defence possible, in case the means by which he hopes to prevent the enemy from reaching us does not succeed?"

Colonel Hendon replied in the affirmative. The question and answer instantaneously reached each invisible member of the Council, as well as the explanations which preceded them.

Number Seven asked how long in his estimation it would take for the people of Frankville to prepare.

The colonel could not say, but it would be advisable to act as if they were to be attacked in a fortnight.

Number Two: "Should we await the attack, or would you think it preferable to prevent it?"

"We must do all in our power to prevent it," answered the colonel; "and if we are threatened with a fleet, we must blow up Herr Schultz's ships with torpedoes."

On this, Doctor Sarrasin offered to call into council the most distinguished chemists, as well as the most experienced artillery officers, and give to them the task of examining the plans which Colonel Hendon had ready to submit to them.

Question from Number One—

"What is the sum necessary for the immediate commencement of the works of defence?"

"We should have at our disposal from fifteen to twenty millions of dollars."

"I propose that the Citizens' Assembly be instantly convoked."

President Sarrasin: "I will put it to the vote."

The bells in each telephone rang twice, announcing that the proposal was unanimously adopted.

It was half-past eight. The Council had only lasted eighteen minutes, and had not disturbed any one.

The popular assembly was convoked by means as simple, and almost as expeditious. Doctor Sarrasin communicated by telephone the vote of the Council to the Town Hall. An electric peal was instantly set in motion at the summit of each of the columns in every square of the city. The columns were surmounted by luminous dial plates, on which the hands, moved by electricity, pointed to half-past eight, the hour for the assembly.

This clamorous call, continuing for a quarter of an hour, brought all the inhabitants out of their houses, they glanced up at the nearest dial, and ascertaining that some national duty required their presence at the Town Hall, they hastened thither as fast as possible.

In less than forty-five minutes the Assembly was complete. Doctor Sarrasin was already in the place of honour, surrounded by the Council, whilst Colonel Hendon waited at the foot of the tribune, until permission was given him to speak.

The greater number of the citizens already knew the reason of the meeting being called. In fact, the discussion of the Civic Council, automatically, stereographed by the Town Hall telephone, had been immediately sent to the papers, printed in a special edition, and placarded all over the town.

The municipal hall was an immense building, roofed with glass, and brilliantly lighted by gas.

The crowd which filled it was calm and orderly, every one standing. All the faces were cheerful. Perfect health, an active and regular life, and a quiet conscience, placed them above any unruly passion of alarm or anger.

At exactly half-past eight, the president rang his bell, and silence fell on the assembly.

The colonel ascended the tribune. There, in sober, but forcible language, without useless ornament or oratorical pretensions—the language of a man, who, knowing what he is talking about, clearly expresses himself—Colonel Hendon related the inveterate hate which Herr Schultz bore against Frankville, Doctor Sarrasin, and his work, and the formidable preparations announced by the *New York Herald*, destined to destroy their city and its inhabitants.

" It is for you to decide what is best to be done," he continued. " Some people, possessing neither courage nor patriotism, might perhaps prefer to give up the land, and leave the aggressors to do what they wish with their new home. But I am certain beforehand that such a pusil-lanimous proposal would find no echo among my fellow-citizens. Men who are able to understand the greatness of the object aimed at by the founders of the model city, men who have accepted its laws, are necessarily men of heart and intelligence. Sincere representatives of pro-gress, you will do everything to save our incomparable town, the glorious monument raised by science, to ameliorate the fallen condition of man ! Your duty, there-fore, is to give your lives for the cause you represent."

Thunders of applause greeted this peroration. Several speakers supported Colonel Hendon's motion.

Doctor Sarrasin, having impressed the necessity of con-stituting a Committee of Defence, which was to take imme-diate measures, with all the secrecy indispensable in military operations, the proposal was adopted.

A member of the Civic Council then suggested that five million dollars should be voted for the works. A show of hands ratified this measure.

At five-and-twenty minutes past ten the meeting was over, and the citizens of Frankville were about to leave the hall, when an unexpected incident occurred. The empty tribune was suddenly occupied by a stranger of most curious appearance. He had sprung up as if by magic. His face showed that he was labouring under frightful excitement ; but his attitude was calm and resolute. His torn and muddy clothes, his bleeding forehead, told of something extraordinary.

At sight of him every one paused. With an imperative gesture, the stranger commanded silence.

Who was he ? Whence had he come ? No one, not even Doctor Sarrasin, ventured to ask him.

" I have just escaped from Stahlstadt," he said. " Herr Schultz had condemned me to death. God has allowed me to reach you in time to attempt to save you. I am not unknown to you all. My venerated master, Doctor Sarrasin, can tell you, I hope, that in spite of my appearance, rendering me unrecognisable even to him, some confidence may be placed in Max Bruckmann ! "

" Max ! " exclaimed both the doctor and Otto at once, starting towards him.

He stopped them by a sign.

Max had been, indeed, miraculously saved. After forcing the grating, just as he was almost suffocated, the current swept him onwards, and two minutes later threw him on the bank, outside Stahlstadt, indeed, but almost lifeless.

For several hours the brave young fellow lay stretched motionless in the darkness, far from all help, on the lonely desert. When consciousness returned, it was daylight. He thanked God that he had escaped from that horrible Stahlstadt! He was no longer a prisoner. The next moment his thoughts were concentrated on Doctor Sarrasin, his friends, and fellow citizens.

"I must save them!" he repeated.

By a supreme effort he got upon his feet. He was thirty miles from Frankville, and he had thirty miles to traverse on foot, for there was no railway in that direction, not even a cart or a horse to be got, for the whole country round the terrible Steel City was shunned. He pressed on, however, without taking a moment's rest, and at a quarter-past ten arrived at the city.

The placards which covered the walls told him all. He found that the inhabitants had been warned of the threatened danger; but they were not aware of its frightful nature, or that it was immediate.

The catastrophe premeditated by Herr Schultz, was to take place on this very evening, at a quarter to twelve. It was now a quarter-past ten.

Max had not a moment to lose, he sped through the

town, and at twenty-five minutes past ten, as the assembly
was about to break up, he scaled the tribune.

"Not in a month, my friends," he cried, "not even in a
week, must you expect the danger! But in an hour, this
awful catastrophe, a rain of iron and fire, will burst upon
your town. An engine, worthy the invention of a fiend,
which will carry thirty miles, is at this very moment
pointed against us. I have seen it. Let the women and
children seek shelter in the deepest and strongest cellars,
or let them instantly leave the town, and take refuge in the
mountains. All the men must prepare to combat the fire
by every possible means. Fire will for the time be your
only enemy. Neither armies nor soldiers will march
against you. The adversary who menaces you disdains all
ordinary modes of attack. If the plans and calculations
of a man, whose power for evil is well known to you, are
realised—unless Herr Schultz is mistaken for the first time
in his life—fire will suddenly break out in at least a hundred
places all over Frankville. We shall presently have to
face the flames at a hundred different points! Whatever
happens, the population must be saved first; such of your
houses and monuments which cannot be preserved, or even
the whole town, time and money can restore!"

In Europe, Max would have been thought mad. But
in America it is not wise to refuse to believe in any
miracle of science, however unexpected; so, by Doctor

Sarrasin's advice, the young engineer was listened to and believed in.

The crowd, awed as much by the accent and appearance of the speaker as by his words, obeyed, without even dreaming of disputing his commands. The doctor answered for Max Bruckmann, and that was enough.

Orders were immediately given, and messengers sent out in every direction.

As to the inhabitants, some withdrew to the cellars of their dwellings, resigned to suffer all the horrors of a bombardment, others on foot, horseback, or in carriages, hastened out into the country, and ascended the steeps of the Cascade Mountains. In the meantime the able-bodied men collected in the square, and in different places pointed out by the doctor, everything that would serve to subdue fire, that is to say, water, earth, and sand.

In the Hall the deliberation continued.

Max was evidently beset by some idea which filled his brain to the exclusion of every other thought. He muttered to himself—

"At a quarter to twelve! Is it really possible that that villainous Schultz will destroy us with his execrable invention ?"

Suddenly Max drew out his pocket-book. He made a gesture requiring silence, and then, pencil in hand, rapidly

put down several figures on one of the pages.   As he did
so his brow cleared, his face became radiant.

" Ah ! my friends !" he exclaimed, " my friends ! Either
these figures are liars, or else all that we fear will vanish
like a nightmare before the evidence of a problem in the
science of projectiles, the solution of which I have till this
moment sought in vain.   Herr Schultz is mistaken ! The
threatened danger is but a dream.   For once, his science is
at fault ! Nothing of what he foretold will come to pass.
It's impossible !   His formidable shell will fly over Frankville without touching it, and if there is anything to fear,
it will be only in the future !"

What could Max mean? His friends did not understand !

The young Alsacian then explained the result of his
calculations.

In his clear ringing voice he explained his demonstra-
tion in such a way as to render it luminous, even to the
most ignorant.   It was light succeeding darkness, calm
following agony.   Not only would the projectile leave
untouched the doctor's city, but it would touch nothing
whatever.   It was destined to lose itself in space !

Doctor Sarrasin acknowledged the correctness of Max's
calculations, and then, pointing to the luminous dial in the
hall—

" In three minutes," he exclaimed, " we shall know

whether Schultz or Max Bruckmann is right! Whatever happens, my friends, we need not regret any of the precautions we have taken, and we still must neglect nothing which can baffle the inventions of our enemy. If his design fails for the present, as Max has just given us reason to hope, it won't be the last. Schultz's hate will never be stifled or arrested."

"Come!" exclaimed Max.

All followed him into the square. Three minutes passed in breathless suspense. The quarter before twelve was tolled forth from the great clock!

Four seconds after, a dark mass was seen high above their heads; quick as thought it rushed onwards, and with a sinister hiss soon disappeared far beyond the town.

"A pleasant journey to it!" shouted Max, with a burst of laughter. "If Herr Schultz's shell keeps up that speed, it will never again fall upon terrestrial soil!"

In two minutes a roar was heard like distant thunder. This was the report of the cannon in the Bull Tower, the sound reaching Frankville a hundred and thirteen seconds after the projectile had passed at the rate of four hundred and fifty miles an hour.

CHAPTER XIII.

NEWS FOR THE PROFESSOR.

" Max Bruckmann, to Professor Schultz, of Stahlstadt.

" Frankville, September 14th.

" I CONSIDER it proper to inform the King of Steel, that on the evening of the day before yesterday, I succeeded in passing beyond the frontier of his dominion, preferring my own safety to that of the model in the blazing workshop.

" While taking leave, I should fail in my bounden duty were I not in turn to reveal my secrets. Do not, however, be uneasy on that account, I shall not require you to pay for the knowledge with your life.

" My real name is not Schwartz, and I am not a Swiss. Alsace is my country, and I am called Max Bruckmann.

" I am a tolerable engineer, if one may take your word for it ; but first and foremost, I am a Frenchman. You

have shown yourself the implacable enemy of my country, my friends, and my family. You have entertained odious designs against everything I hold most dear. I have dared, and done all, in order to discover those designs ; I will dare and do all to frustrate them.

"I hasten to let you know that your first shot has failed to take effect.

"It has not hit the mark, for, thank heaven, it could not. Your gun is not the less a wonderful one, though the projectiles which it sends forth will never do any harm to any one! They will fall nowhere. I had a presentiment of this, and, to your great glory, it is now an established fact, that Herr Schultz has invented a wonderful cannon, entirely inoffensive.

"You will hear with pleasure that we saw your perfect shell, at forty-five minutes and four seconds past eleven, pass above our town. It was flying towards the west, circulating in space, which it will continue to do until the end of time. A projectile, animated with an initial speed twenty times superior to the actual speed, being ten thousand yards to the second, can never fall! This movement, combined with terrestrial attraction, destines it to revolve perpetually round our globe.

"You ought to have been aware of this

"I hope and expect that the cannon in the Bull Tower is quite spoilt by this first trial; but two hundred thousand dollars is not too much to have paid for the pleasure of having endowed the planetary world with a new star, and the earth with a second satellite.

"MAX BRUCKMANN."

An express was immediately sent from Frankville to Stahlstadt with this letter; and Max must be forgiven for not having been able to resist the satisfaction of writing it to Herr Schultz.

Max was quite right when he said that the famous shell would never again fall on the surface of the earth, and also right when he predicted the cannon of the Bull Tower would be rendered useless by the enormous charge of pyroxile.

The receipt of this letter greatly discomfited Herr Schultz, and was a terrible shock to his self-love. As he read it, he turned perfectly livid, and his head fell on his breast as if he had been struck with a club. He remained in this state of prostration for a quarter of an hour. When he revived his rage was frightful. Arminius and Sigimer alone witnessed the outbursts !

However, Herr Schultz was not a man to acknowledge himself beaten.

Henceforth the struggle between him and Max would continue to the death. He still had other shells charged with liquid carbonic acid, which less powerful, but more practical guns, could throw to a short distance.

Calming himself by an effort, the King of Steel re-entered his study, and continued his work.

It was clear that Frankville, now more than ever menaced with danger, must neglect nothing by which it could be put into a perfect state of defence.

CHAPTER XIV.

CLEARING FOR ACTION.

ALTHOUGH the danger was no longer imminent, it was serious. Max communicated to Doctor Sarrasin and his friends all that he knew of Herr Schultz's preparations, and described his engines of destruction. On the next day the Council of Defence, in which he took a principal part, occupied itself with discussing a plan of resistance, and preparing to put it into execution.

In all this Max was well seconded by Otto, whom he found altered in character, and much improved.

No one knew the details of the resolutions passed. The general principles alone were regularly communicated to the press. It was not difficult to trace in them the practical hand of Max.

"In preparing for defence," said the townsfolk, "the great thing is to know the strength of the enemy, and adapt the system of resistance to that strength. No doubt, Herr Schultz's cannon are formidable, but it is better to have to face these guns, of which we know the number, calibre, range, and effect, than to have to combat unknown engines."

It was decided to prevent the investment of the town, either by land or sea.

How this was best to be done was a question actively discussed by the Council, and the day on which a placard announced that this problem was solved, no one doubted it. The citizens hastened *en masse* to execute the under- taking. No tasks were despised which could contribute to the work of defence. Men of all ages, and of every position in life, became simple labourers on this occasion, and everything went on rapidly and cheerfully. Pro- visions sufficient for two years were stored in the town. Coal and iron also were brought in considerable quanti- ties ; the iron, being requisite for manufacturing arms of all sorts, and the coal absolutely necessary, both for warmth, and for fuel to work the various warlike engines it was intended to employ.

In addition to the heaps of iron and coal could be seen gigantic piles, composed of sacks of flour, and quarters of smoked meat, stacks of cheeses, mountains of preserved and dried vegetables, all stored in the market places. Numbers of sheep and cattle were also enclosed in the beautiful gardens of the town.

When the decree appeared for the mobilisation of all men able to carry arms, the enthusiasm with which it was received, testified to the excellent disposition of these soldier-citizens. Plainly dressed in woollen shirts, cloth trousers and half-boots, strong leather caps, and armed with Werder rifles, they drilled every day in the avenues.

Gangs of coolies banked up earth, dug trenches, raised intrenchments and redoubts at every favourable point. The casting of guns had been commenced and pushed on with activity, for the numerous smoke furnaces in the city were easily transformed into casting furnaces.

Max was indefatigable in all this. He was here, there, and everywhere in the thick of all the work. Did some theoretical or practical difficulty arise, he could immediately solve it. If necessary, he turned up his sleeves and gave a practical definition. His authority was always accepted without a murmur, and his orders punctually attended to.

Next to him, Otto did his best. Although at first he had thought of ornamenting his uniform with gold lace, he soon gave up the idea, seeing that to set a good example to others he must be content to do the duty of a simple soldier.

He, therefore, took his place in the battalion assigned to him, and conducted himself like a model soldier. To those who at first attempted to pity him, he replied—

" Every one according to his merits. Perhaps I should not have been able to command! The least I can do is to learn to obey ! "

A report—which turned out to be false—gave a still more lively impulse to the works of defence. Herr Schultz, it was said, was negotiating with some maritime company for the transport of his cannon. From that time these sort of hoaxes were the order of the day. Now it was that the Schultz fleet was off the coast of Frankville, and now that the Sacramento Railway had been cut by Uhlans, who had apparently dropped from the clouds.

But all these rumours, which were immediately contradicted, were invented by the correspondents of newspapers, hard up for matter to fill their despatches, their object being to sustain the curiosity of their readers. The truth was that Stahlstadt did not give the least sign of life.

This perfect quietude, although it left Max ample time to complete his preparations, caused him a good deal of uneasiness in his rare moments of leisure.

" Is it possible that the ruffian has changed his tactics, and is preparing some new mode of attack ? " he thought.

However, the plans for checking the advance of the enemy's ships, and preventing the investment of the town, promised to answer well, and Max redoubled his exertions.

His sole pleasure and only rest, after a hard day's work,

was the short hour which he passed every evening in Madame Sarrasin's drawing-room.

From the first, the doctor had stipulated that he should always come and dine at his house, unless he was prevented by another engagement; but, by some singular circumstance, no other invitation enticing enough to make Max give up this privilege had as yet presented itself.

The everlasting game of chess between the doctor and Colonel Hendon could not have been sufficiently interesting to explain the punctuality with which he presented himself every day at the door of the mansion. We are therefore compelled to believe that there was another attraction for Max, and we might, perhaps, have suspected its nature, although, assuredly, he did not as yet suspect it himself, had we observed the interest which he took in the conversations between himself, Madame Sarrasin, and Mademoiselle Jeannette, when they were all three seated near the large table, at which the two ladies were working at what might be necessary for future service in the ambulances.

"Will these new steel bolts be better than those of which you showed us a drawing?" asked Jeannette, who was interested in everything connected with the defence.

"No doubt about it, mademoiselle," replied Max.

"Ah, I am very glad of that! But how much trouble

and research is represented by the smallest industria'
particular. You told me that five hundred fresh yards of
the trench were dug yesterday? That is a great deal, is
it not?"

"Indeed, no, it is not nearly enough. At that rate we
shall not have finished the enclosure at the end of a
month."

"I should much like to see it done, and these horrible
Schultz people arriving! Men are very fortunate in being
able to work and make themselves useful. Waiting is
never so trying for them as for us, who are of no use."

"Of no use!" exclaimed Max, usually so calm, "no use!
And for whom do you think do these brave men, who
have left everything to become soldiers, for whom do they
work, if not to secure the safety and happiness of their
mothers, their wives, and those whom they hope may
become their wives? From whence comes their ardour, if
not from you, and to what would you trace this readiness
to sacrifice themselves, if not——"

Here Max got rather confused, and stopped. Mademoiselle Jeannette did not urge him, and good Madame
Sarrasin herself was obliged to close the discussion by
saying to the young man that a love of duty was doubtless
sufficient to explain the zeal of the greater number.

And when Max, at the call of inexorable duty, tore
himself away from this pleasant talk, in order to finish a

plan, or an estimate, he carried with him the invincible determination to save Frankville and its inhabitants.

Little could he conjecture what was about to happen, and yet it was but the inevitable result of a state of things so utterly unnatural as this concentration of all power in a single person, which was the fundamental principle in the City of Steel.

CHAPTER XV.

THE EXCHANGE OF SAN FRANCISCO.

THE Exchange of San Francisco, by which term is expressed, as it were algebraically, immense industrial and commercial business, presents one of the strangest and most animated scenes in the world.

The geographical position of the capital of California imparts to its Exchange, as a natural consequence, the cosmopolitan character, which is one of its most remarkable features.

Beneath its handsome red granite porticoes, the tall, fair Saxon jostles the slight, active dark-haired Celt. The negro meets the Finlander and the Hindoo.

The Polynesian gazes with astonishment at the Greenlander. The Chinaman, with oblique eyes and long plaited pigtail, endeavours to outdo in trade his historic enemy the Japanese.

Every tongue, every dialect, every jargon mingles there as in a modern Babel.

On the 12th of October this place of business opened in the usual way. At about eleven o'clock the principal brokers and men of business began to arrive, accost one another gravely or gaily, according to their several tempers, shaking hands, and going together to the refreshment bar to fortify themselves by "liquoring up" for the operations of the day.

One after the other went to open the little metal door of the numbered letter-boxes, which in the vestibule received the correspondence of subscribers. Enormous packets of letters were drawn forth, and eagerly examined.

In a short time the market prices for the day were announced, when the crowd gradually increased. Groups more or less numerous were formed, from among which arose a murmur and hum of human voices.

Then commenced a shower of telegraphic messages from all quarters of the globe.

Scarcely a minute passed that the officials of the Exchange did not add a fresh strip of blue paper to the collection of telegrams placarded on the north wall, which was read forth in a stentorian voice, amid the now deafening buzz.

The commotion and hubbub went on increasing.

Clerks rushed in and out; the telegraph office was

besieged; messages sent out, answers received every instant.

All note-books were open, entries made, erased, or torn up.

At about one o'clock a contagious excitement appeared to take possession of the crowd. A mysterious sensation passed like the trembling of an earthquake through these agitated groups of human beings.

A piece of news, startling, unexpected, and incredible had been brought by one of the partners in the Bank of the Far West, and it circulated with the rapidity of an electric flash.

Exclamations and comments were heard on all sides.

"Impossible! It's a trick—a hoax," said some. "Who is likely to believe anything so preposterous?"

"Well," said others, "there may be something in it. No smoke without fire, you know."

"But is a man in his position likely to fail?"

"People in apparently the very best positions fail."

"But, sir," cried one, "the fixtures, tools and engines alone represent more than eighty million dollars!"

"Without reckoning the cast iron and steel, raw material, and manufactured articles!" added another.

"To be sure! That's just what I say, too! Schultz is good for ninety millions of dollars, and I'll undertake to be answerable for that on his demand!"

"Well, but then how do you explain this suspension of payment?"

"Explain! I don't explain it at all! I don't believe it!"

"Don't you? As if such things did not happen every day to houses of the most firm and established reputations!"

"Stahlstadt is not a house; it is a city."

"Of course! It is perfectly impossible it can have broken up so completely. A company will certainly be formed to carry on the business."

"But why on earth did not Schultz form such a company instead of declaring himself bankrupt?"

"Exactly, sir; and there's the absurdity! So absurd that the statement won't bear examination. It is neither more nor less than a pure fabrication, probably invented by Nash, who is desperately anxious for a rise in steel."

"A fabrication? False intelligence? Nothing of the sort! Schultz has not only failed; he has absconded!"

"Come! Come!"

"Absconded, sir! The telegram announcing it has this moment been posted up!"

A formidable wave of humanity rolled towards the frame in which the despatches were placarded.

The last strip of blue paper bore these words:

"New York, 12.40.—Central Bank. Manufactory of Stahlstadt. Stopped payment. Liabilities, as far as

known : forty-seven million dollars.   Schultz has disappeared."

There was now no doubt about the truth of the astounding
intelligence ; and conjectures and rumours were rife.

By two o'clock lists of failures consequent upon that of
Schultz began to pour in.

The Mining Bank of New York lost most.

The firm of Westerly and Son at Chicago was implicated
to the extent of seven million dollars.

The house of the Mitwaukees of Buffalo, five millions.

The Industrial Bank of San Francisco, a million and
half.

The names of numbers of minor firms followed with
proportionate losses.

But, without waiting for this news, came the natural
rebound.

The money market, which was so dull in the morning,
was now not steady for two hours together.   What
starts! what rises! what fluctuations, what unrestrained
speculation!

A rise in steel, and going up every minute; a rise in
coal ; a rise in the shares of all the foundries in the
American Union ; a rise in the products of every kind of
iron industry ; a rise in Frankville land.

Although on the declaration of war the latter had fallen
to zero, and disappeared from the list of quotations, it

had now suddenly risen to a hundred and eighty dollars an acre.

In the evening the newspaper shops were perfectly besieged. But though the *Herald*, the *Tribune*, the *Alta*, the *Guardian*, the *Echo*, and the *Globe* printed in gigantic characters the meagre information they had been able to collect, it after all amounted to very little.

All that was known was, that on the 25th of September, a draft for eight millions of dollars, accepted by Herr Schultz, drawn by Jackson, Elder, and Co., of Buffalo, having been presented to Schring, Strauss, and Co., the King of Steel's bankers, in New York, those gentlemen had stated that the balance to their client's account was insufficient for such an enormous sum, and had telegraphed this to him, without receiving any answer.

On referring to their books, they perceived with consternation that for thirteen days no letter and no bills had come from Stahlstadt.

From that moment drafts and cheques, drawn by Herr Schultz on their bank, came in daily, to undergo the fate of being returned with the words, no funds.

For four days inquiries, telegrams, and furious questions rained from one side on the bank and then again on Stahlstadt.

At last a decisive reply was given.

" Herr Schultz disappeared on the 17th of September "

so said the telegram.   "No one can throw the least light
on this mystery.   He has left no orders, and the coffers in
every section are empty."

Since then it had been no longer possible to conceal the
truth.   Many of the principal creditors had taken fright
and sent in their claims to the commercial court.   Ruin
spread rapidly in all directions.

At twelve o'clock, on the 13th of October, the total
amount of failures was estimated at forty-seven millions of
dollars.   When everything became known it was likely to
amount to sixty millions.

This was all that could be said, and all that the journals,
with a few exceptions, could report.   Of course they
announced for the next day full and special particulars,
"as yet unpublished."   And, indeed, to do them justice,
each, within an hour of the first announcement, had
despatched a correspondent on the road to Stahlstadt.

By the evening of the 14th of October, Steel City was
besieged by an army of reporters, all with open note-books,
and pencils in hand.   Like a wave, however, they broke
against the outer wall, for the sentries were in their places,
and any attempt to bribe or soften them was utterly in
vain.

They, nevertheless, ascertained that the workmen as yet
knew nothing, and that the routine of the sections in nothing
had been changed.   The overseers had merely announced

the day before by superior order, that no funds nor instructions had been issued from the Central Block, and
that in consequence the works would be suspended the
following Saturday, unless contrary orders were received.

All this only complicated, instead of throwing any light
on the situation.

That Herr Schultz had disappeared for nearly a month ,
of that there was no doubt.   But what might be the cause
and import of this disappearance no one knew.   A vague
impression that the mysterious personage might at any
moment re-appear still prevailed, and seemed to lessen the
general uneasiness.

For some days all work had gone on as usual.   Every
one had pursued his task within the limited horizon of his
section.   The salaries were paid from the strong boxes
every Saturday, and the principal coffer had met all
local necessities.   But centralisation had been brought to
too high a pitch of perfection in Stahlstadt ; the master
had reserved so absolutely to himself the superintendence
of everything, that his absence could not fail in a very
short time to cause a stoppage in the machinery.   Thus,
from the 17th of September, the day on which the King
of Steel had signed his orders for the last time up to the
13th of October, when the news of the suspension of
payment had burst like a thunder-clap, millions of letters,
a large number containing considerable bills, passed through

the Stahlstadt Post Office, had been deposited in the box
of the Central Block, and no doubt had reached Herr
Schultz's study. But he alone had the right to open them,
mark them with a red pencil, and transmit them to the
principal cashier.

Even the highest functionaries in the town never dreamt
of doing anything out of their regular department.

Invested with almost absolute power over their subordi-
nates, they were each, in connection with Herr Schultz—
as they were also with his memory—like so many instru-
ments, without authority, without power of initiating, or
a voice in any matter. Each fortified himself within the
narrow limits of his commission, waited, temporised, and
watched the course of events.

The end came at last. This remarkable state of
affairs was prolonged until the principal houses interested,
suddenly seized with a panic, telegraphed, begged for an
answer, entreated, protested, and finally commenced legal
proceedings. This took some time. No one was willing
hastily to suspect that prosperity, so firmly believed in, had
been resting on an insecure basis. But the fact was now
patent : Herr Schultz had fled from his creditors.

This was all that the reporters could gather. The
celebrated Meiklejohn himself, famous for having extracted
a political avowal from President Grant, the most taciturn
man of his time; the indefatigable Blunderbuss, remarkable

for being the first, although but a simple correspondent of
The World, to announce to the Czar the news of the
capitulation of Plevna, even these great men in the re-
porting line had not this time been more fortunate than
their brethren. They were forced to confess to themselves
that *The Tribune* and *The World* could not yet give the
latest news of the bankrupt Schultz.

That Stahlstadt was indeed in a strange situation will
be seen when it is remembered that it was an independent
and isolated town, permitting no regular and legal inquiry.
Herr Schultz's signature was, it is true, protested at New
York, and his creditors had every reason to believe that
the stock and manufactory would indemnify them in some
degree.

But to what court should they apply to obtain an
execution or a sequestration ? Stahlstadt lay in a territory
of its own, where everything belonged to Herr Schultz.

If only he had left a representative, an administrative
council, or a substitute. But there was nothing of the sort.
He himself was king, judge, general-in-chief, notary, lawyer,
and the only commercial court in the city.   In his person
he had realised the ideal of centralisation.

Therefore, he being absent, there was absolutely no one
in power, and the whole fabric fell like a house of cards.

In any other situation, the creditors would have been
able to form a syndicate, substituting themselves for Herr

Schultz, lay hands on the stock, and take the direction
of affairs.   To all appearance only a little money and
regulating power was needed to set the machine to work.

But nothing of this was possible.   The proper legal
instrument to effect this substitution was wanting.   There
was a moral barrier round the City of Steel, which was if
possible more insurmountable than its walls.   The unfortunate creditors could see the securities for their debts,
though quite unable to touch them.

All they could do was to unite in a general assembly,
and agree to address a request to the Congress to ask it to
take their case in hand, espouse the interests of its natives,
pronounce the annexation of Stahlstadt to American
territory, and thus include this monstrous creation in the
common laws of civilisation.   Several members of the Congress were personally interested in the business, the request
was tempting to the American character, and there was
reason to believe that it would be crowned with complete
success.

Unfortunately the Congress was not then in session, so
that a long delay was to be feared before the matter could
be submitted to it.

Until that time nothing could be done in Stahlstadt, and
one by one the furnaces were extinguished.

The consternation among the population of ten thousand
families who lived by the manufactory was profound.   But

what were they to do? Continue to work in hopes of
wages, which might be six months in coming, or might
never come at all? No one was inclined to adopt this
opinion. Besides, what work could they do? The source
from which orders came was dried up as well as everything
else. All Herr Schultz's clients waited the legal solution.
The heads of the sections, engineers, and overseers, could
do nothing for want of orders.

Numberless assemblies, meetings, and debates took
place, though no plan could really be fixed on. The
enforced stoppage soon brought with it a train of misery,
despair, and vice. As the workshops emptied, the public-
houses filled. For each chimney which ceased to smoke
in the factory, a tavern sprung up in one of the neighbouring villages.

The wisest and most prudent among the workmen, those
who had foreseen hard times, and had laid by for a rainy
day, hastened to escape with bag and baggage; and
happy rosy-cheeked children, wild with delight at the
new world revealed to them, peeped through the curtains
of the departing waggons, loaded with their father's tools
and furniture, and the precious bedding, dear to the heart
of the housewife. These all were scattered east, south,
and north, soon finding other factories, other anvils, other
hearthstones.

But for one who could thus depart, there were ten whose

poverty nailed them to the soil! There they remained, hollow-eyed and broken-hearted! Selling their poor garments to the flock of birds-of-prey in human shape, whose instinct attracts them to scenes of great disasters, reduced to the last extremities in a few days, deprived of credit as well as of wages, of hope as well as work, and seeing before them a future of misery as black and dismal as the fast approaching winter!

CHAPTER XVI.

A BRACE OF FRENCHMEN CAPTURE A TOWN.

WHEN tidings of the disappearance of Schultz reached Frankville, Max's first words were—

" Suppose it should be merely a trick !"

He reflected, however, that the results to Stahlstadt had been so disastrous as to make such an hypothesis inadmissible.

Still, as hatred is an unreasoning passion, the exasperated rage of such a man as Herr Schultz might really render him capable of sacrificing everything to it. Whether or not this was the case, it was undeniably necessary to be on the " *qui vive.*"

The Council of Defence immediately, therefore, issued a proclamation exhorting the inhabitants to be on their guard against false reports spread by the enemy, with the object of lulling them into security.

Frankville judged it prudent to continue all the preparations for defence, taking no notice of what might after all prove to be a stratagem of its arch-enemy.

But by-and-by the journals of San Francisco, Chicago, and New York published further details, and news of the financial and commercial consequences of the Stahlstadt catastrophy, forming altogether a mass of evidence to prove that Schultz was a genuine bankrupt, and had indeed disappeared.

And so, one fine morning, the doctor's model city became aroused to the fact that it was safe, just as a sleeper escapes from the oppression of a horrible dream by the simple operation of awaking.

Yes! Frankville was clearly out of danger, without having to strike a blow, and Max, now absolutely certain of it, announced the news amid public rejoicing.

A strain seemed suddenly removed. The public drew, as it were, a long sigh of relief, and assumed a holiday aspect.

Everybody shook hands, offered mutual congratulations, and invited each other to dinner. All the women came out in fresh toilettes, and the men took leave of drill, manœuvres, and hard work.

Every one went about looking satisfied, and beaming. Frankville was just like a town peopled with convalescents. But among them all, the happiest was unquestionably Doctor Sarrasin.

The worthy man had felt himself responsible for the
fate of those who had come with confidence to settle on his
territory, and to place themselves under his protection.

For the last month, the fear of having allured them to
destruction, when he had only sought their happiness, had
never left him a moment's rest. Now he was released from
terrible anxiety, and breathed freely.

This common danger had more closely united the
citizens. All classes had been brought nearer to each
other, and knew themselves brothers, animated with the
same feelings, and affected by the same interests. A
new sensation had sprung up in the hearts of all.
Henceforward the inhabitants had a strong feeling of
patriotism for Frankville. They had feared, they had
suffered for their town, and now they knew how much
they loved it.

The material results of having placed it in a state of
defence were also to the advantage of the city. Their
strength was known. They felt more sure of themselves,
and would now be ready for whatever the future might
bring.

The prospects of Doctor Sarrasin's work had never
appeared more brilliant ; and (a rare thing) no ingratitude
was shown towards Max. Although the safety of the
population had not been his work, public thanks were
voted to the young engineer, as to the organiser of the

defence, the man to whose devotion the town would have owed its safety, had the plans of Herr Schultz succeeded.

Max, however, did not regard his part as finished. The mystery surrounding Stahlstadt might still, he thought, conceal danger. He could not rest satisfied until he had thrown complete light into the very midst of the darkness which still enveloped the City of Steel.

He resolved, therefore, to return to Stahlstadt, and to stop at nothing until he had probed the last secret to its depths.

Doctor Sarrasin represented to him that the enterprise would be difficult, that it would bristle with dangers, that he knew not what mines might spring beneath his feet, and that, in fact, it would resemble a descent into the lower regions. Herr Schultz, such as he had been described to him, was not a man to disappear with impunity to others, or to bury himself alone beneath the ruins of all his hopes. They had every reason to fear the last desperate design of such a man. It would be like the terrible dying agony of a shark!

"My dear doctor, it is just because I think all you imagine possible that I believe it my duty to go to Stahlstadt," answered Max. "The place may be compared to a shell from which I must snatch the match before it bursts, and I will even ask your permission to take Otto with me."

" Otto !" exclaimed the doctor.

"Yes! He is now a fine fellow, who may be relied on ; and I assure you that this excursion will do him a great deal of good !"

"May God protect you both !" returned the old man, fervently grasping his hand.

The next morning a carriage drove through the deserted villages and deposited Max and Otto at the gate of Stahlstadt.

Both were well equipped, well armed, and very determined not to come back until they had cleared up the mystery.

They walked side by side along the outer road which led round the fortifications, and the truth, which Max till then had persisted in doubting, now lay before them.

It was evident that the place was completely deserted. From the lonely road, which he now trod with Otto, he could formerly have seen within the town flaring gas, or the flash of a sentinel's bayonet, and many other signs of life. The windows of the different sections would have been illuminated and dazzling. Now all was gloomy and silent. Death seemed to hover over the city, its tall chimneys standing up like skeletons. The footfalls of Max and his companion alone aroused the echoes of the place. The sensation of solitude and desolation was so strong that Otto could not help remarking—

ENTERING STAHLSTADT.   [*Page* 207.

"It is singular, but I have never felt silence similar to this! We might suppose ourselves in a cemetery!"

It was seven o'clock when Max and Otto reached the edge of the moat, opposite to the principal gate of Stahlstadt. Not a living creature appeared on the crest of the wall, and of the sentinels who formerly had stood at equal distances all round, like so many human posts, not one remained. The drawbridge was raised, leaving before the gate a gulf from five to six yards in width.

It took them more than an hour before they could succeed in fastening the end of a stout rope, by throwing it with all their might, so as to catch over one of the beams. After much trouble, Max managed it, and Otto going first, drew himself up hand over hand to the top of the gate. Max passed up to him their arms and ammunition, and then he himself took the same way.

They now carried their rope to the other side of the wall, let down all their impedimenta, and finally slid down themselves.

The two young men were now on the roundway which Max remembered having followed the first day he entered Stahlstadt. Complete silence and solitude were all around. Before them rose, black and dumb, the imposing mass of buildings which glared with their thousand glass windows at the intruders, as if to say—

"Be off! You have no busin ss to attempt the penetration of our secrets!"

Max and Otto consulted.

"We will assail the O gate, as th at is the one with which I am best acquainted," said Max.

They bent their steps westward, a d soon arrived before the monumental arch, which bore on its front the letter O. The two massive oaken doors, full of great iron nails, were closed. Max approached, and struck them several times with a large stone taken from the road.

The echo alone resounded.

"Come! to work!" he cried to Otto.

They had now to recommence the troublesome work of throwing their rope over the door, until it met with some obstacle on which it would firmly catch. This was difficult, but they succeeded at last, and Max and Otto surmounted the wall, and found themselves in section O.

"What a nuisance!" exclaimed Otto, looking round; "where is the use of all our trouble? We have made but little progress! No sooner have we got over one wall, than we find another before us!"

"Silence in the ranks!" returned Max. "Here we are in my old workshop. I am not sorry to see it again, that we may possess ourselves of certain tools which we shall be sure to need, not forgetting a few packets of dynamite."

As he spoke they entered the great casting-hall, to which

the young Alsacian had been admitted on his arrival at
the factory.

How dismal it now looked, with its furnaces extinguished,
its rails rusted, its dusty cranes extending their gaunt arms
in the air, like so many gallows.   All this struck a chill to
the heart, and Max felt that some diversion to their ideas
would be pleasant.

"Here is a workshop which will interest you more," he
observed, leading the way to the canteen.

Otto followed obediently, and showed unmistakable
signs of satisfaction as he caught sight of a whole regiment
of red, yellow, and green bottles, drawn up in order of
battle on a wooden shelf.   Several boxes of preserved
meats and other good things were also there; more than
enough to furnish them with a substantial breakfast, the
want of which they began to feel, so, having spread
the food on the counter, the two young men fell to.

Whilst eating, Max considered what was next to be
done.   There was no use in even thinking of scaling the
wall of the Central Block, as it was prodigiously high,
isolated from all the other buildings, and without a projec-
tion on which to fasten a rope.   To find the door—of
which there was probably only one—it would be necessary
to go through all the sections, anything but an easy task.
Dynamite could be used, though that was dangerous, for
it seemed impossible that Herr Schultz should have

disappeared without constructing traps in his deserted territory, or establishing counter-mines to the mines which those who wished to take possession of Stahlstadt would not fail to form. But no fear of this could deter Max.

Seeing that Otto was now refreshed and rested, Max went with him to the end of the road which formed the axis of the section, up to the foot of the huge freestone wall.

"What say you to attempting a blast here?" he asked. "Shall we pierce the wall and lay a train of dynamite?"

"It will be hard work, but we are not afraid of that!" replied Otto, ready to attempt anything.

They first had to lay bare the foot of the wall, then introduce a lever between two stones, loosen one, and finally, with a drill, pierce several little parallel trenches. By ten o'clock all was prepared, the dynamite in its place, and the match lighted.

Max knew that it would burn for five minutes, and as he had noticed that the canteen was underground, and was a regular stone-vaulted cellar, he took refuge there with Otto.

Suddenly every building, and even the cellar, were shaken as if by an earthquake. Then, almost immediately, a tremendous roar, resembling the sound of three or four batteries thundering at once, rent the air.

In two or three seconds a perfect avalanche of stones

and débris showered down far and wide. Then began an uproar of breaking roofs, crashing beams, falling walls, mingled with the sound of a cascade of broken glass.

When the frightful din had ceased, Max and Otto ventured forth from their retreat.

Accustomed as he was to the terrific effects of an explosion, Max was perfectly astonished at the results of this one. Half of the section had been blown up, and the dismantled walls of all the neighbouring workshops resembled those of a bombarded town. On all sides the ground was strewed with heaps of rubbish, and pieces of glass and plaster, whilst clouds of dust settling down, fell like snow on the ruins.

Otto and Max hastened to the inner wall.

From fifteen to twenty feet of it had been thrown down, and on the other side of the breach, the ex-draughtsman of the Central Block could see the well-known hall, where he had passed so many monotonous hours.

As the place was no longer guarded, it was soon entered.

Still the same silence everywhere.

Max passed in review the studios, where formerly his comrades admired his diagrams. In one corner he discovered the very half-sketched drawing of a steam-engine on which he had been engaged when Herr Schultz summoned him to the park. In the reading-room lay the papers and familiar books.

Everything bore the look of business suspended, of a sudden interruption to work.

The two friends had now reached the inner limits of the Central Block and stood before the wall, which Max believed divided them from the park.

"Are we to make this fellow dance too?" asked Otto.

"Perhaps; but first we can look for a door, which a simple fusee could send flying."

They proceeded, therefore, to skirt the wall around the park, from time to time making a détour to avoid a building jutting out like a spur, or to climb a fence. But they never lost sight of it, and were soon rewarded for their trouble, by coming to a low, narrow door.

In two minutes Otto had bored a gimlet hole through the oaken panels, and Max, applying his eye to the opening, perceived with lively satisfaction that on the other side lay the tropical park, with its eternal verdure and summer temperature.

"One more door to blow up, and we shall be in the place!" he exclaimed to his companion.

"A fusee for a piece of wood like this would be too great an honour," returned Otto.

And as he spoke he struck a heavy blow on the postern with an axe he carried.

It had not begun to give way, however, when they heard a key turned, and two bolts slipped back.

The door half opened, though held inside by a thick chain.

"Wer da?" (Who goes there?) demanded a hoarse voice.

CHAPTER XVII.

PARLEY BEFORE THE CITADEL.

THE two young men were little prepared for such a question.   It astonished them more than if they had been met by a rifle shot.

Max had had a great many conjectures about this mysterious town, and the very last thing he had expected was that a living being would quietly demand the reason of his visit.   His enterprise, legitimate enough, under the supposition that Stahlstadt was completely deserted, assumed quite another aspect, when the city was found still to be inhabited.

That which in the one case was but a kind of archæological inquiry, in the other became an attack by force of arms, and bore the character of a burglary.

These reflections rushed in upon the mind of Max with such force that he stood as if struck dumb.

"Who goes there?" repeated the voice, impatiently.

There was certainly some reason for impatience. For intruders to have reached this door by overcoming so many obstacles, scaling walls, and blowing up half the town, and then to have nothing to say on being simply asked, "Who goes there?" was somewhat astonishing.

In half a minute Max became aware of the awkwardness of his position, and he replied in German—

"Friend or enemy, whichever you like! I wish to speak to Herr Schultz."

Directly he uttered these words an exclamation was heard from the other side of the door—

"Ach!"

And through the opening Max could discern a red whisker, half a bristly moustache, and a dull eye, which he immediately recognised as belonging to Sigimer, one of the uncouth beings who had been ordered by Schultz to guard him.

"Johann Schwartz!" exclaimed the giant, with a sort of stupid joy, "Johann Schwartz!"

The unexpected return of his prisoner seemed to astonish him as much as his mysterious disappearance must have done.

"Can I speak to Herr Schultz?" repeated Max, finding that this exclamation was the only answer he received.

Sigimer shook his head.

"No order!" he said. "Can't come in here without an order!"

"At least you can tell Herr Schultz that I am here, and want to see him."

"Herr Schultz not here!   Herr Schultz gone!" replied the giant, with a shade of sadness in his tone.

"But where is he?   When will he be back?"

"Don't know!   Instructions remain as before!   No one can enter without an order!"

These disjointed sentences were all that Max could get from Sigimer, who to any other questions maintained a dogged and obstinate silence.

Otto at last became impatient.

"Where's the use of asking permission to enter?" said he.   "It is much easier to take it!"

And he shoved against the door to try and force it open. It was held by the chain, however, and a more powerful arm than his soon shut it, and rapidly drew the bolts.

"There must be several men behind there!" cried Otto, rather humiliated at this result.

He applied his eye to the gimlet-hole, and uttered a cry of surprise.

"There's a second giant!"

"Arminius, no doubt," returned Max, in his turn putting his eye to the hole.

"Yes!   It is Arminius, Sigimer's companion."

As he spoke, another voice, apparently from the sky, caused Max to raise his head.

"Wer da?" it said.

This time it was Arminius who spoke, looking over the top of the wall, which he had reached by means of a ladder.

"Come, you know well enough who it is, Arminius!" returned Max. "Will you open, yes or no?"

These words had scarcely left his lips when the muzzle of a gun was pointed over the wall, and a bullet just grazed the brim of Otto's hat.

"Very well, here's an answer for that!" exclaimed Max, who, placing some dynamite under the door, blew it into fragments.

A breach being thus made, Otto and Max, their guns in their hands, and their knives between their teeth, sprang into the park.

The ladder still leant against the now tottering wall, and at its foot were traces of blood, but neither Arminius nor Sigimer were there to bar the progress of the adventurers.

The gardens lay before them in all the richness of their vegetation.

Otto was delighted.

"What a magnificent place!" he said; "but look out! We had better proceed like sharpshooters! These sour-

krout-eaters are most likely watching for us—hiding
behind the bushes !"

Max and Otto separated, and each taking one side
of the walk which opened before them, they advanced
cautiously from tree to tree, from mound to mound, after
the most approved principles of strategy.

This was a wise precaution. They had not gone a
hundred yards when a second shot was heard, and the
bark of the tree Max had just quitted flew in splinters.

"This is serious! Down on the ground!" ejaculated
Otto.

And, adding example to precept, he crawled on hands
and knees up to a thorny thicket bordering the square, in
the centre of which rose the Bull Tower.

Max, not following this advice quickly enough, narrowly
escaped another bullet, and only avoided a fourth by
darting behind the trunk of a palm-tree.

"Fortunately these fellows shoot no better than raw
recruits!" called out Otto to his friend.

"Hush!" returned Max. "Don't you see the smoke
hanging about that window on the ground-floor? The
villains are in ambush there! But I mean to play them a
trick in my turn!"

In a trice, Max had cut a good-sized stick from the
shrubbery, on which he hung his coat, placing his hat on
the top. Having thus improvised a very presentable

MAX AND OTTO FIGHTING THE GIANTS.   [*Page* 219.]

dummy, he stuck it in the ground, so that the hat and sleeves alone were visible, then, gliding up to Otto, he whispered in his ear—

"Just keep them amused by firing at the window, first from your place and then from mine! I'm off to take them in the rear!"

And Max, leaving Otto to skirmish, crept cautiously away through the bushes.

A quarter of an hour passed, whilst about twenty shots were exchanged without result on either side, though Max's coat and hat were completely riddled with bullets. As to the window-blinds, Otto's gun had sent them into shivers.

Suddenly the firing ceased, and Otto distinctly heard a stifled cry of—

"Help! help! I've got him!"

To leave his shelter, fly through the shrubbery, and spring in at the window, took Otto but a moment.

Struggling desperately on the floor, entwined like two serpents, were Max and Sigimer. Surprised by the sudden attack of his adversary, who had forced an inner door, the giant had been unable to use his weapons. But his herculean strength rendered him a formidable enemy, and although thrown to the ground, he had not lost hope of gaining the upper hand. Max, on his side, displayed remarkable vigour and agility.

The fight would certainly have terminated in the death of one of the combatants, had not Otto's intervention made a less tragic end possible. The two together soon disarmed Sigimer, and bound him so that he could move neither hand nor foot.

"Where's the other fellow?" asked Otto.

Max pointed to the further end of the room, where Arminius lay bleeding on a bench.

"Has he been shot?" he asked.

"Yes," replied Otto.

Together they examined the body.

'Quite dead!" said Max.

'If so the rascal might have died in a better cause!" exclaimed Otto.

"Here we are, masters of the place!" said Max. "So now to serious business. Let us first explore the study of the great Herr Schultz!"

From the room, in which the last act of the siege had been performed, the two young men proceeded through the suite of apartments which led to the sanctum of the King of Steel.

Otto was lost in admiration at the sight of such splendour.

Max smiled as he looked round at him, and opened, one after the other, the doors of the magnificent rooms, till they reached the green-and-gold apartment.

He had expected to find something new, but nothing so
strange as the spectacle which here lay before their eyes.
It looked just as if the General Post-Office of New York
or Paris had been robbed and its contents thrown pell-mell
on the floor. On every side were heaps of letters and
sealed packets, on the writing-table, on the chairs, on
the carpet. They waded knee-deep in a flood of papers.
All the financial, industrial, and personal correspondence
of Herr Schultz, brought to the letter-box in the park wall,
and faithfully carried in by Arminius and Sigimer, had
here accumulated in their master's study.

How many questions, what expectations, what anxious
suspense, what misery and tears were enclosed in those
voiceless envelopes addressed to Herr Schultz! What
millions of money, too, no doubt, in paper, cheques, bills,
and orders of all sorts!

Everything rested here motionless through the absence
of the only hand which had a right to break these fragile
but inviolable seals.

"We have now," said Max, "to discover the secret door
of the laboratory!"

He began by taking all the books out of the bookcase.
This was useless; he could not find the masked passage he
had traversed in company with Herr Schultz.

In vain he shook the panels one by one, and, with an
iron rod, which he took from the mantelpiece, tapped

them in succession ! In vain he struck the wall in the
hope of hearing it give forth a hollow sound ! It was
very evident that Schultz, uneasy at no longer being the
sole possessor of his secret, had done away with that
door.

He must necessarily have opened another.

" But where ?" asked Max. " It must be here somewhere,
as Arminius and Sigimer have brought the letters to this
room, which Herr Schultz doubtless continued to use after
my departure. I know enough of his habits to be sure
that, after bricking up the old passage, he would wish to
have another close at hand, and concealed from inquisitive
eyes ! Can there be a trap-door under the carpet ?"

The carpet itself showed no signs of a cut ; but none the
less was it unnailed and raised. The floor, examined bit
by bit, showed nothing suspicious.

" How do you know the opening is in this room at all ?"
asked Otto.

" I am morally certain of it !" answered Max.

" Then the ceiling only remains to be explored," returned
Otto, springing on to a chair.

His idea was to get up to the lustre and sound the
central rose with the butt end of his gun.

However, no sooner had he grasped the gilded chan-
delier, than, to his extreme surprise, it sunk under his
hand. The ceiling opened and left to view a wide gap,

from which a light, self-acting steel ladder slid down level with the floor.

It was a distinct invitation to ascend.

" Here we are! Come along!" said Max, composedly, and immediately began to mount the ladder, closely followed by his friend.

CHAPTER XVIII.

THE KERNEL OF THE NUT.

THE top of the steel ladder was fixed close to the wall of a vast circular chamber, there being no communication with the exterior.   It would have been in complete darkness had it not been for a dazzling white light which streamed through the thick glass of a bull's-eye, fixed in the centre of the oak floor.   For purity and brilliancy it might be compared to the moon, when she is in her full beauty.

Perfect silence reigned within these mute and eyeless walls.   The two young men imagined themselves in the antechamber of a tomb.

But before bending over the glass, Max hesitated for a moment.   He had attained his object !   The secret, to penetrate which he had come to Stahlstadt, was about to be revealed to him !

This feeling, however, soon passed off.   Together he and

Otto knelt beside the disc and looked down into the chamber beneath.

A horrible and unexpected sight met their astonished gaze.

The glass disc, being convex on both sides, formed a lens, which immensely increased in size all objects seen through it.

Here was the secret laboratory of Herr Schultz. The intense glare which shone through the disc, as if from the lantern of a lighthouse, came from a double electric lamp, still burning in its airless bell, being incessantly fed by a powerful voltaic pile.

In the middle of the room, motionless as marble, and enormously magnified by the refraction of the lens, a human form was seated.

Pieces and splinters of shells were strewn on the ground around this spectre.

There was no doubt about it! It was Herr Schultz himself, recognisable by his horrid grinning mouth, and his gleaming teeth ; but a gigantic Herr Schultz, suffocated and frozen by the action of a terrible cold, caused by the explosion of one of his frightful engines of warfare.

The King of Steel was seated at his table, holding an enormous pen like a lance in his hand, as if he were writing. Had it not been for the stony glare of his dilated eyeballs, and his set mouth, he would have appeared still

living.   Here this awful corpse had been for a month,
hidden from all eyes, and now discovered like a mammoth
which has been concealed for ages in the glaciers of
the Polar regions.   Everything around him was frozen, the
re-agents in their jars, the water in its receivers, and
the mercury in its reservoirs !

In spite of the horror of this spectacle, Max's first
thought was one of satisfaction that they had been
fortunate enough to be able to observe the interior of the
laboratory from the outside, for if he and Otto had entered
they must infallibly have been struck dead.

Max soon guessed how the fearful accident had occurred,
when he marked that the fragments scattered on the ground
were small pieces of glass.   He knew that the inner case of
Herr Schultz's suffocating projectiles contained liquid
carbonic acid, and that, to resist the enormous pressure, it
was formed of tempered glass, which has ten or twelve
times the ordinary strength ; the great fault of this newly-
invented production, however, is that, by some mysterious
action, it often suddenly bursts without any apparent reason.
This was evidently what had happened.   Perhaps the
interior pressure had helped to provoke the explosion of
the shell deposited in the laboratory ; at any rate, the
discharged acid, on returning to a gaseous state, had
occasioned a fearful lowering of the surrounding atmosphere,
even to a hundred degrees below zero.

The effects had indeed been something awful. Death had surprised Herr Schultz in the attitude he was in at the time of the explosion, and in a moment he was turned into ice.

One circumstance which Max particularly noticed, was that at the time of his death the King of Steel was engaged in writing.

What was inscribed on the sheet of paper lying beneath that lifeless hand? It would be interesting to know the last thought, and read the last words of such a man.

The difficulty was to procure the paper. The idea of breaking the disc so as to descend into the laboratory could not be entertained for an instant. The gas would have immediately rushed out and suffocated every living being. The risk of bringing a sudden death upon themselves could not be run merely for the sake of satisfying their curiosity. Max, therefore, seeing that the writing as well as everything else was so wonderfully magnified and brilliantly illuminated, endeavoured to read it from a distance. Being well acquainted with the handwriting of Herr Schultz, with a little trouble he at last made out the following lines.

According to the usual custom of Herr Schultz, it was rather an order than an instruction.

" Order to B. K. R. Z. to advance the projected expedition against Frankville by a fortnight. As soon as this order is received execute the measures I have devised ;

they must this time be overwhelming and complete. Do not alter an iota of what I have decided upon. I wish that in a fortnight Frankville should become a city of the dead without a surviving inhabitant. I hope for a modern Pompeii, to be at once a terror and an astonishment to the whole world. If my orders are properly executed, this result will be inevitable.

"You will send the bodies of Doctor Sarrasin and Max Bruckmann to me. I wish to have them.

"Schult——."

The signature was unfinished, the final z and the usual flourish being wanting.

Max and Otto gazed mute and motionless at this strange spectacle, feeling as if they were witnessing the invocation of some malignant genius.

But it was time to leave the dismal scene, and the two friends, agitated by conflicting feelings, descended from the room above the laboratory.

There, in that dark tomb, for, when the electric current failed, the lamp would be extinguished, the corpse of the King of Steel would remain alone, dried up like a mummy Pharaoh, whom twenty centuries had not reduced to dust!

An hour later, having unbound Sigimer, who seemed puzzled to know what to do with his liberty, Otto and Max quitted Stahlstadt, and took their way back to Frankville, which they entered the same evening.

Doctor Sarrasin was busy in his study when the return of the two young men was announced to him.

" Tell them to come in !" he exclaimed. " Come in quickly !"

" Well ?" said he, as soon as the friends presented themselves before him.

" Doctor," replied Max, " the news we bring from Stahlstadt will put your mind at rest for a long time.   Herr Schultz is no more ! Herr Schultz is dead !"

" Dead !" exclaimed Doctor Sarrasin.

The good man remained thoughtful for a few moments, without uttering another word.

" My dear fellow," he said at last, " can you understand that this news, which ought to make me rejoice, since it takes from us the dread of the thing I most execrate, war, and the most unjust, unreasonable war ever heard of !—can you understand how, against all reason, it makes my heart ache ?   Oh, why should a man of such powerful intelligence have constituted himself our enemy ?   Why did he not use his rare intellectual qualities for the benefit of his fellow creatures ?   How much wisdom has been lost, which would have been so valuable, had it been associated with us, and used for a common object !   All this at once struck me when you said : ' Herr Schultz is dead ;' but now tell me all that you know of this unexpected event."

" Herr Schultz," replied Max, " has met his death in the

mysterious laboratory, which, with such diabolical ingenuity, he had striven to render inaccessible to all others. No one but himself ever knew of its existence, and no one consequently could penetrate into it to bring him help. He has fallen a victim to that marvellous concentration of all his plans in his own hands, on which he had so erroneously relied. By the will of Providence, his desire of being himself the key to all his projects, has been turned to his own destruction!"

"It could not have been otherwise!" answered Doctor Sarrasin. "Herr Schultz started with a totally wrong notion. For, indeed, is not the best government the one of which the chief, on his death, can be most easily replaced, and which will continue to work smoothly, just because all the machinery is open and visible?"

"You will see, doctor," said Max, "how all that has happened in Stahlstadt bears out what you have said. We found Herr Schultz seated before his desk, that central point whence came all those orders so implicitly obeyed by the Steel City, and which no one ever dreamt of disputing. Death had left him every appearance of life, so that for a moment I thought the spectre would have spoken to us! But the inventor has fallen by his own invention! He was killed by one of the shells, with which he hoped to destroy our town, just as he was signing his name to the order for our extermination! Listen!"

And Max read aloud a copy he had taken of the horrible words written by Herr Schultz.

Then he added—

"The greatest proof of the death of Herr Schultz, even if we had not seen him, is that everything around him has ceased to live. There is nothing breathing in Stahlstadt. As in the palace of the Sleeping Beauty, slumber has suspended all life, and arrested every movement. The effects of the master's death has extended, not only to the servants, but also to the machinery."

"Yes," returned Doctor Sarrasin; "we see in this the justice of God! From indulging in his hatred against us, and urging on his attack with such boundless rancour, Herr Schultz has perished."

"That is true," answered Max; "but now, doctor, let us leave the past and think only of the present. Although the death of Herr Schultz gives peace to us, it causes the ruin of the wonderful business he created. Blinded by his success, and his hatred of France and you, he had supplied large numbers of cannon and weapons to any one who might be our enemy, without getting sufficient guarantees. In spite of this, and although the payment of all his debts would take a long time, I believe that a strong hand could set Stahlstadt on its legs again, and turn to a good purpose all that has been hitherto used for an evil one. Herr Schultz has only one likely heir, doctor, and that is you.

His work must not be allowed to fall to the ground entirely. It is too much the belief of this world that the only profit to be drawn from a rival force is in its total annihilation. This is not really the case, and I hope you will agree with me that, on the contrary, it is our duty to endeavour to save from this immense wreck all that can be used for the benefit of humanity. Now, I am ready to devote myself entirely to this task."

"Max is right," said Otto, grasping his friend's hand, "and here am I, ready also to work under his orders, if my father will give his consent."

"I certainly approve, my dear lads," replied Doctor Sarrasin. "Yes, Max, there will be no want of capital, and, thanks to you, I shall hope to have in the resuscitated Stahlstadt such an arsenal that no one in the world will ever henceforth dream of attacking us! And as we shall then be the strongest, we must at the same time endeavour to be also the most just, we must spread the benefits of peace and justice all around. Ah, Max! what enchanting dreams! And when I feel that, with you to help me, I can at least accomplish a part, I ask myself why—yes, why have I not two sons! Why are you not the brother of Otto! We three working together, it seems as if nothing could be impossible!"

CHAPTER XIX.

A FAMILY AFFAIR.

PERHAPS in the course of this veracious narrative we have not been sufficiently communicative about the personal history of those who have played such prominent parts in it. We may now, therefore, be allowed to stop in order to give a few details regarding them.

It must be acknowledged that the good doctor was not so entirely taken up with the idea of collective humanity, as to merge in it the welfare of individuals. He had, therefore, been struck by the sudden pallor which overspread the countenance of Max as he uttered his last words. He sought to read in the young man's eyes the cause of this sudden emotion. The silence of the older man seemed to question the engineer, as if he expected him to speak, but Max, mastering himself with a strong effort, immediately resumed his composure. His complexion reassumed its natural tint, and his attitude was merely that of a man who expects the continuance of an interesting conversation.

Doctor Sarrasin, slightly provoked at this evidently assumed calmness, approached his young friend, and with a familiar gesture, laid his hand upon his wrist, just as he would on that of a patient, whose pulse he wished quietly, unobtrusively to feel.

Max allowed this naturally without apparently noticing the doctor's intentions, and as he did not open his lips—

" My dear Max," observed the old man, " we will put off our conversation about the future destiny of Stahlstadt to some other time. For although we are vowed to the work of labouring to ameliorate the condition of mankind, it is not forbidden us also to occupy ourselves with the fate of those we love, of those who are nearest to us. Well, I think the time has come to tell you what a young lady, whose name I will mention presently, replied not long ago to her father and mother, when for the twentieth time that year they had been asked for her in marriage.

" The proposals were, for the most part, such that even the most fastidious could have had no reason for refusing them, and yet this young woman always said ' No !'

At this point Max drew his hand away with a sudden movement from the doctor's grasp, and the latter, as if he was satisfied on the subject of his patient's health, and had not noticed that both his arm and his confidence had been withdrawn, quietly continued his story.

"'Well, now,' said the mother, to the young lady of whom I speak, 'just tell me the reason of these continued refusals. Education, fortune, position, good looks, all are there. Why this decided no, so resolute and prompt, to requests which you don't even take the trouble to consider a little? You are not usually so very peremptory!'

"At this the girl determined to speak clearly and frankly, and thereupon replied—

"'I say no with as much sincerity as I would say yes, dear mother, if the yes came really from my heart. I agree with you that several of the matches you have proposed to me are perfectly unexceptionable; but, besides my belief that most of those addresses were paid more to what is considered the best, that is the richest match in the town, than to me myself, and that that idea does not incline me to say yes, I will venture to tell you, since you wish it, that none of these proposals is the one I hope for, the one that I still expect, and which, unfortunately, I may have to wait a long time for, if it ever comes at all!'

"'What, my dear,' said the mother, in surprise, 'you ——'

"She did not end that sentence, for want of knowing how to finish it, and in perplexity turned to her husband, with looks which plainly begged for help and advice.

"However, as he did not intend to interfere in the discussion between the mother and daughter until a little more light had been thrown on the subject, he put on an obtuse air, and counterfeited so well that the poor girl, blushing with embarrassment, and perhaps with a little anger, suddenly determined to make a clean breast of it.

" ' I said, dear mother,' she continued, ' that the proposal I hoped for might be a very long time in coming, and might possibly never come at all. I add that this delay, although so indefinite, will neither hurt nor astonish me. I have the misfortune to be very rich ; he, whose proposal I hope for, is very poor ; therefore, he will not make it, and he is right. It is for him to wait——'

" ' Why not for us to speak,' said the mother, wishing, perhaps, to prevent her daughter from uttering words she feared to hear.

" Then the husband interposed.

" ' My dear,' he said, affectionately, taking his wife's hands in his, ' it is not with impunity that a mother, reverenced by her daughter as you are, can constantly in her presence sing the praises of a fine, handsome fellow, who, ever since she was born, has been almost one of the family, that she remarks to every one on the solidity of his character, that she glories in what her husband says, when he has occasion in his turn to boast of his remarkable intelligence, or speaks feelingly of the thousand proofs of devotion he has received from him! If the girl who saw this young man, distinguished both by her father and her mother, had not admired him herself, she would have failed in her duty!'

"'Oh, father!' cried the girl, throwing herself into her mother's arms, to hide her confusion, 'if you guessed, why did you make me speak!'

"'Why?' returned the father, 'why, but to have the joy of hearing you, my darling, that I might be still more certain that I was not mistaken, to be able at last to tell you that both your mother and I approve your choice, that your heart has been given where we wished; and to spare a poor and proud man from making a proposal, at which he feels a reluctant delicacy, I will do it myself—yes, I will do it, because I have read his heart as I have read yours! Calm yourself then! On the first favourable opportunity, I will ask Max, if, by any possibility, he would care to become my son-in-law!'"

Taken unawares by this sudden peroration, Max had started to his feet as if moved by a spring. Otto silently grasped his hand, while Doctor Sarrasin held out his arms. The young Alsacian was pale as death. But does not happiness sometimes take this appearance when it enters without warning into a strong heart!

CHAPTER XX.

CONCLUSION.

FRANKVILLE, released from all anxiety, in peace with its neighbours, well governed, happy, thanks to the good behaviour of its inhabitants, is highly prosperous. Its success is so justly merited that it causes no envy, and its strength enforces the respect even of the most warlike.

Under the iron rule of Herr Schultz, the City of Steel was a terrible manufactory, an organised source of destruction ; but, thanks to Max Bruckmann, the liquidation of its debts was effected without loss to any one, and Stahlstadt became a centre of production, unsurpassed by any other industry.

A year ago, Max became the happy husband of Jeannette, and the birth of a child has recently added to their felicity.

As to Otto, he worked gallantly under his brother-in law's directions, and seconded all his efforts. His sister is hoping soon to see him married to a friend of hers, whose good sense will preserve her husband from any relapse.

The wishes of the doctor and his wife are thus fulfilled, and to put it in a few words, they are at the zenith of happiness and even of glory—if glory ever entered into the programme of their honest ambitions.

We may now be assured that the future belongs to the efforts of Doctor Sarrasin and Max Bruckmann, and that the example of Frankville and Stahlstadt, as model city and manufactory, will not be lost upon future generations.